Amber pressed the

The tree lit up in a daz~~~~
with fireworks going of~~ ~~~ ~~~~ ~~~ ~~~~~ ~~~
aahs, a sharp crack punctured the air. Monty's mind
registered the danger as reflex took over.

A gunshot.

"Get down! Gunfire!" Monty was already up the stairs
and bolting across the stage.

Pop! Pop!

Monty lunged for Amber and threw her to the ground
behind the podium, pinning her underneath him to
protect her.

The sound of the shots echoed in his head. He
remained in that position, shielding her, waiting,
listening.

"Monty, I need to move," she said in a strained
breath, like he was crushing her.

He didn't realize he'd put so much of his weight on
her and rolled off. "Stay down." He peered out from
behind the podium, looking to see if the gunman was
still out there.

Then it occurred to him that with all the accusations
and hateful glares, whoever had opened fire had
probably been targeting him.

WYOMING CHRISTMAS CONSPIRACY

JUNO RUSHDAN

Harlequin

INTRIGUE

For Amber M., a caring, dedicated educator. While you were the principal at my children's elementary school, you became one of my personal heroes. Thank you for your service.

ISBN-13: 978-1-335-45709-7

Wyoming Christmas Conspiracy

Copyright © 2024 by Juno Rushdan

Recycling programs for this product may not exist in your area.

Harlequin Enterprises ULC
22 Adelaide St. West, 41st Floor
Toronto, Ontario M5H 4E3, Canada
www.Harlequin.com

Printed in Lithuania

MIX
Paper | Supporting responsible forestry
FSC® C021394

Juno Rushdan is a veteran US Air Force intelligence officer and award-winning author. Her books are action-packed and fast-paced. Critics from *Kirkus Reviews* and *Library Journal* have called her work "heart-pounding James Bond-ian adventure" that "will captivate lovers of romantic thrillers." For a free book, visit her website: www.junorushdan.com.

Books by Juno Rushdan

Harlequin Intrigue

Cowboy State Lawmen: Duty and Honor

Wyoming Mountain Investigation
Wyoming Ranch Justice
Wyoming Christmas Conspiracy

Cowboy State Lawmen

Wyoming Winter Rescue
Wyoming Christmas Stalker
Wyoming Mountain Hostage
Wyoming Mountain Murder
Wyoming Cowboy Undercover
Wyoming Mountain Cold Case

Fugitive Heroes: Topaz Unit

Rogue Christmas Operation
Alaskan Christmas Escape
Disavowed in Wyoming
An Operative's Last Stand

Visit the Author Profile page at Harlequin.com.

CAST OF CHARACTERS

Monty Powell—This part-time rancher and full-time state trooper refuses to let anyone else decide his destiny. Accused of murder, he must rely on help from his family and someone he least expected—the woman he let walk away years ago.

Amber Reyes—After Monty broke her heart, she left home and became a teacher. When her father's funeral brings her back, she is determined to prove the innocence of the only man she's ever loved.

Chance Reyes—Amber's brother and Monty's close childhood friend. He's also a lawyer with a secret that will change many lives.

Hannah Delaney—A strong-willed detective who must find balance between doing her job and maintaining her loyalty to her fiancé's family, the Powells.

Erica Egan—This journalist will cross any line for a scoop and to see her name in the byline.

Waylon White—Not thrilled to partner with Hannah Delaney, this detective won't do any favors for the Powell clan.

Holly Powell—Monty's mother and mayor of the town.

Chapter One

Friday, December 6
7:35 a.m.

Amber Reyes sped down the snow-covered road, clenching the steering wheel so tight her fingers grew numb. Even though it was freezing outside—30 degrees, which wasn't too bad for December in Wyoming—she was hot under the collar and not from the heat blasting out of the vent in her 4x4. She was headed to her half sister's place.

A half sister whose existence she hadn't been aware of until August, at the reading of her father's will when the details of a legal trust he'd established had been explained. Amber, along with everyone else in the small town, knew of Pandora Frye—the beautiful, eccentric, arrogant, wild child.

But she'd been shocked to discover Pandora was also the beautiful, eccentric, arrogant, illegitimate child of Carlos Reyes, the product of an extramarital affair twenty-two years ago.

Amber believed her mother had never known that her father had cheated. They'd always had a loving, picture-perfect marriage until her mother died ten years ago of cancer. Then everything had changed. At nineteen, Amber had learned the people closest to her couldn't be trusted.

Primarily her father. So she'd run from home to make her

own way in the world. And that was before she found out about her half sibling.

A decade later, she hadn't thought her father could top his previous conniving efforts to manipulate her into an arranged marriage—much less from the grave.

How wrong I was.

Though her father had bequeathed Amber most of the land, including the valuable river that ran through it, and the cattle, he had also stipulated ironclad conditions for her to receive it. The betrayal, his indomitable will to have things his way continued after his death.

But then came the real shocker. Her father had not only named Pandora in his living trust, claiming her as his daughter, but he had also given her the Reyes family home and one acre of land surrounding it, which she'd take ownership of at the beginning of the new year following his death. Giving Amber and her brother, Chance, one final holiday season in their home.

Thinking about it made Amber's blood boil. The house her parents had been married in. The house she and her brother had been born in. Land they had been raised on. The house that had been in the family for generations would soon belong to a virtual stranger.

Not if I have anything to say about it.

A wave of nausea swept over her. Slowing down and keeping her eyes on the road, she kept driving as she unzipped her purse in the passenger seat of her Jeep Wrangler. Inside the handbag, her fingers skimmed over the unopened letter from her father, but she didn't find what she was looking for. The saltine crackers were probably still sitting on the kitchen counter. She'd been in such a rush to speak with her sister— *half sister*—that she'd forgotten them.

Maybe she should've listened to her brother and stayed home. But that was the problem. If she didn't convince Pandora to sell them the house and the acre of land around it, she and Chance wouldn't have a family home for much longer.

Her cell phone rang. The caller ID showed up on the Bluetooth screen on the dash. Sometimes she thought she had a psychic link with her big brother.

She hit the Accept button, putting the call on speaker in the rugged SUV. "What is it? I'm almost there."

"You forgot your crackers."

Despite her anger, she smiled. "I just realized. I'm pretty nauseous."

"Pregnancy will do that to you," Chance said.

She put a hand to her belly. Only four months along, but if not for the baggy sweaters she'd started wearing, the rounded bump that had emerged one morning like magic would be visible to everyone. One careless, reckless night, swamped by grief, she'd given in to a moment of weakness and slept with Montgomery Powell. "We agreed not to use the P-word."

"Which one, Pandora, pregnancy or Powell? I can't keep track."

"Don't use any of them," she demanded, putting both hands back on the wheel. Best for things to be simple.

"You're going to have to tell Monty sooner or later. I think you should've done it by now."

"Thankfully it's not up to you and I choose later." *Much, much later.* "This is my body, my timeline. I won't be harassed or bullied by Monty or his family or you."

"Okay." Chance's snippy tone signaled he thought she was making a mistake.

Her death grip on the steering wheel made her forearms cramp. "I'd like to put out one dumpster fire before dealing with the next."

She switched on the wipers to prevent the falling snowflakes from sticking to the windshield. This time of year, it was typical to get several inches. She'd been gone so long, she'd forgotten how early the winter storms started here in Wyoming, in the valley where the small towns of Laramie and Bison Ridge were nestled.

"You're wasting your time," Chance said.

"I am not. She agreed to hear my proposal." Pandora, the leech, just as vicious as her mother, Fiona, had texted last night, telling Amber to come by for coffee at ten this morning. With flagrant disregard to the fact that Amber was filling in as a substitute teacher at the local elementary school and class started at nine. She had been up since five and decided to throw the young woman off-balance by showing up early. Inappropriately early. Outright rude, truth be told, but Amber didn't care.

"Only to see your face when she rejects it. The girl was over the moon at the reading of the will and so was her mother. The house isn't worth much, but she was ecstatic to get her grubby hands on it because it's ours. Or was. At least Dad left you everything of value with the land and cattle."

Everything but only one way to keep it, or lose all that, too, to Pandora.

"With that unconscionable proviso," she said through gritted teeth. "Why aren't you fuming? He left you nothing."

"Dad set me up for success. He paid for my bachelor's and law degrees, and I didn't have to work through school. I was able to focus on being the top of my class and got hired by a powerhouse company."

In a way, Chance was right. The day he started practicing, he did so debt-free. Not many of his colleagues had the privilege to say the same. Now he worked for Ironside Protection Services, earning a high six-figure salary, which was substantial compared to what she made as a schoolteacher.

A profession she'd chosen out of desperation after she fled the ranch, but surprisingly a rewarding one. "Still, he shouldn't have left you nothing."

"The simple watch he wore every day and his old rodeo buckles aren't nothing. They meant a great deal to him. Besides, I read the letter he wrote for me. I'm at peace with his decision. You should read yours. It might change how you feel."

Glancing at her purse, she seethed. "I have half a mind to burn mine."

"You'd regret it. Just like you're about to regret seeing Pandora."

She sighed, hoping he was wrong. For once. Though Chance seldom was. A fact that grated on her like sandpaper scraping her skin. "I'm almost at the harpy's abode. I'll call you afterward to tell you how it went." A long breath eased from her tight throat as she let up a bit on the accelerator.

"Don't bother calling me back. But would you mind grabbing us breakfast from Divine Treats? I'll take a bear claw. Also, one of those savory croissants. Ham and cheese."

Amber pulled up to the block of a recently constructed town house complex, consisting of ten units, in the center of downtown Laramie. Why their father had felt the need to buy Pandora one of these sleek, newly built places as well as give her the family home, too, was beyond Amber. She'd been here once after the funeral, in a failed attempt to get to know the young woman better. The finishes were top-notch, with custom cabinets and furnished with whimsical luxury. Stunning eye candy filled the interior. Their father had spared no expense.

"Don't you want the details on the meeting?" she asked.

"You can wait until you get home to fill me in," Chance said. "That way I can say *I told you so* to your face."

Shaking her head with irritation, she drove around the back to the parking lot. "You're unbelievable. Instead of being the annoying, know-it-all big brother, why can't you—" She lost the power of speech for a moment as her gut clenched.

"Amber? Are you all right? What's wrong?"

She slammed on the brakes, fixing her attention on the vehicle parked beside Pandora's sporty car behind her unit.

"Monty's truck is here." The words left a foul taste in her mouth.

For him to be here at seven forty-five in the morning could only mean one thing. He'd spent the night.

"Are you sure?" Chance sounded skeptical. "At least half the guys in town probably drive a Ford F-150."

She stared past the swirls of white flakes in disbelief at the truck. "How many drive one that's antimatter blue and has the vanity plate PWEL3?"

Buck Powell had a similar plate with the number one. Holly, domestic goddess extraordinaire and now mayor, had the designation number two. Their eldest son had the plate Amber was staring at right now.

Chance swore.

"That calculating, spiteful…" Amber swallowed the ugly words dancing on her tongue. "Is this the reason she agreed to meet me? Only to rub my face in the fact that she's bedding Monty."

"You're so early. Maybe it's coincidence." Her brother's words were comforting, but his tone full of doubt.

Unexpected tears filled her eyes. She didn't know what hurt more, her heart or her pride. "How could he?" she asked, her voice cracking.

"Not to sound like a callous guy on this one, but you two hadn't seen each other for almost ten years. You came home for the funeral, still angry over how things imploded between you two, and had a one-time slipup with him. Four months ago, might I add? You've avoided him ever since then, right?"

"Yeah, I guess so." Even though Monty had called, asking to see her, she'd rebuffed his attempts at contact because she didn't trust his motives and she didn't trust herself around him. With the unalterable stipulation in her father's living trust—Amber had to marry Monty within five months of her dad's death and stay hitched for two years, or everything, the entire property, the cattle, the money, went to Pandora—how could she believe anything he said? Especially if it was all the things her heart longed to hear.

"Plus," Chance added, "Pandora is easy on the eyes and comes across as, quite frankly, a floozy. It's probably nothing more than a one-night stand."

"But he didn't simply have sex and leave." Which would have been bad enough. "He spent the night." *With Pandora!*

Amber had only had the pleasure of a few nights with Monty herself. Even a lifetime ago, before she learned the horrible truth about why he'd taken a sudden interest in her, he had never stayed and cuddled until the sun came up with her.

She squeezed her eyes closed and saw Montgomery Beaumont Powell, six feet three inches of pure sex appeal. Tawny hair, the same as his father's. Intense brown eyes. A strong jaw with the perfect amount of stubble all the time, like he didn't even have to try. And a sweeping landscape of muscle. His sculpted physique was created by hard work on his family's ranch that was adjacent to hers, in addition to the extra effort he put into staying fit for his full-time job with the state police as a trooper. With his swagger and confidence, the man could've been a Hollywood heartthrob. Women swooned after him from Laramie to Jackson Hole. Not only for his heartbreaker looks, but also his status as heir apparent to the Powell fortune.

And Pandora Frye had sunk her claws into him.

The woman was taking everything that didn't belong to her.

Amber opened her eyes. She stared at the antimatter blue truck parked beside the cherry red Alfa Romeo Stelvio and slapped the steering wheel, letting a small scream slip.

"Get a grip," her brother muttered. "It's only sex. Even if he spent the night."

"He can sleep with whomever he likes. Except for her!" She whisked the tears from her eyes. *I will not cry.* Stupid hormones. "This may be a small town, but I'm sure there are tons of women willing to crawl into bed with him." Monty had never had a problem in that department. "He didn't have to sleep with *her*." The living embodiment of her father's broken marital vow. The woman who would move into her family's house. "Yes, she's classically beautiful and nubile—" in fact, they were exact opposites: Pandora was slender, sophisticated, with creamy skin and red hair, whereas Amber was curvy and simple, and a brunette with brown skin "—but he knows something like this would bother me."

More like wound her to the marrow.

"Getting upset won't solve anything. You need to calm down, Tinker."

Tinker Bell. How she despised the nickname. It stopped being cute once she'd turned thirteen. At twenty-nine, it made her sound as ridiculous as she felt being back home. Still pining for Monty Powell, the veritable Peter Pan, who was only interested in using her for her pixie dust.

Straightening, she threw the truck in Park, blocking Monty's and Pandora's vehicles. No quick, clean exits for either party. "You're right. It doesn't matter what they do."

"It really doesn't so long as you marry Monty in twenty-nine days."

The five-month deadline was creeping up on her. One dumpster fire at a time, starting with this. "I'll show Pandora and him that I don't give two figs they're sleeping together. I just need her to agree to sell us back the house," she said in a voice so strained she almost didn't sound like herself.

"You're not still going in there, are you?"

Amber grabbed her purse, slinging it over her shoulder. "I most certainly am. I'm done running from things. This time I'm going to confront it head-on."

"Says the woman running from telling the father of her child that she's four months pregnant and wearing baggy clothes to conceal her burgeoning bump."

"Instead of lecturing me—"

"Reasoning with you."

She huffed. "You should be supporting me."

"You mean enabling you to make poor choices you'll regret."

Why was it so hard for him to be in her corner for once? "Before you can try to talk me out of it, I'm hanging up." She jabbed the red icon, ending the call.

Killing the engine, she pressed her door open against the frigid thrust of the wind. Another thing she'd forgotten about home: it was the second windiest state in the country. The town was in the perfect, or worst, spot depending on perspective. Rather than the mountains surrounding the valley blocking the wind, they made the jet stream faster. Add in high pressure from the Great Basin and low pressure from the plains and the town got squeezed, making the winters harsh.

Cold slapped her face as she climbed out. Icy flakes stung her cheeks. Crisp, clean air moved in the blustery wind, smelling of winter and snow and pine. Zipping up the oversize coat she'd recently purchased to hide that she was expecting, she marched up to the back door. Beside it a sign on the window read Pandora's Box Photography.

Her half sister was a glamour and boudoir photographer. The profession seemed better suited for a big city, but when one's father paid for their lifestyle in hush money, Amber supposed it didn't matter whether their career was profitable.

Bitterness welled inside her. She struggled to tamp it down. Since the day she left home, she hadn't taken one cent from her father or even spoken to him. Everything she had she'd earned and paid for herself, on a meager teacher's salary.

The name, *Pandora's Box*, was apropos, considering the

seven deadly sins seemed tied to the woman. She was the product of lust, had seduced Monty—unless there was some other explanation for him being here—was envious of their status as legitimate Reyes offspring and had, driven by greed, held on to their family home. The Reyes home.

What great evil was next?

Amber raised her fist, wanting to bang out her frustration rather than ring the bell, and knocked—only once because the door swung open on contact.

It must've been slightly ajar. She hadn't noticed. A gust of wind sprayed snow inside the entrance.

"Pandora!" she called out, crossing the threshold. She closed the door, keeping more cold air and snow from seeping in.

Music came from the first-floor bonus room Pandora used as her photography studio. A sultry Kacey Musgraves song just ended and a soulful one by Shawn Mendes started as Amber stood there.

A hopeful thought sprang to mind. Maybe Monty was here for some other reason. To get a portrait taken.

But at seven something in the morning with soft pop music playing?

Hope quickly withered. In its place, anxiety swelled, twisting through her.

Amber had no claim on Monty and no longer wanted any. Not after he'd deceived her right along with her father.

Only the house matters right now.

The door to the studio was cracked open. "Pandora!"

Still no answer. Hesitating at the entrance, Amber braced to encounter some tawdry scene inside, the two of them asleep or, worse, intimate. She set her mind to show no reaction.

Steeling her spine, she pushed on the door and strode inside.

She faltered to a stop and gasped. The blood in her veins froze, her stomach giving an acid twinge. A familiar copper scent wafted in the air.

Monty lay, utterly still, on his stomach on a curved, emerald colored velvet sofa, wearing nothing but black boxer briefs. His eyes were closed, his face slack. One long, muscular arm hung off the side, his knuckles on the floor.

A knife. An open butterfly knife was beside his hand. Covered in blood.

Her breath hitched in her lungs, but she forced herself to breathe as she shifted toward her half sister.

Pandora was sprawled on the floor in the center of the room, eyes frozen open and vacant, expression locked in an unnatural contortion, bruises on her pale face, her throat slit.

Squeezing her eyes shut, Amber turned away. Her mind spun. Steadying herself, she looked over the room.

Clothes were scattered about as though they had undressed in a hurry.

A bottle of whiskey was open on a side table next to the sofa along with a tumbler half-full of liquor. Another was broken on the floor. Lines of white powder were on a small mirror on top of a speaker from which music poured into the room.

Alcohol. Drugs.

Murder.

Sickening dread pooled in her chest.

This couldn't be happening, but it was. Blackness edged her vision and she swayed. For a second, she stood there, hyperventilating. Shaking. Trying to make sense of the sordid, horrible scene.

Grim urgency punched through the paralyzing fear. "Monty?" Why wasn't he moving? Was he dead, too?

Please be alive.

Snapping into action, she rushed to him. Red-lipstick kiss marks were on his cheek and neck. Along with some kind of rash. Hands trembling, she tugged off one of her leather gloves and pressed two fingers to the side of his throat.

He had a pulse. Thready and slow. But he was alive.

There was a strange sound. Was it coming from him?

She tipped her ear closer to his mouth. A wheeze came from him on every exhale.

Amber had never seen him like this, blacked out, wheezing, with a rash. What was wrong with him? And what had happened here?

Her gaze dropped to the bloody knife near his hand and then she looked back at Pandora.

Nausea churned her stomach. Amber had wanted this young woman out of her life from the second she became aware they were related, but not like this. Not murdered, dead, at twenty-two.

This was awful. She needed to call the police. Report it, and say what?

Monty was many things—a liar, a manipulative womanizer— but every cell in her body, every instinct in her gut, told her that he was not a killer.

She'd known him her entire life, once adored him, had kissed him, made love to him, created a baby together and still cared for him far more than she wanted to admit.

In spite of how this looked, and it did look as though he had killed Pandora, Amber knew he wasn't capable of such a thing.

She crouched beside the curved sofa and cupped his face, gripping his chin. "Monty." When he gave no response, she shook his shoulder. "Wake up."

Moaning, he stirred slightly.

"Monty!" She gave him a harder shake, rolling him onto his side. The wheeze became more pronounced and the rash covered his torso. "Please, wake up," she said, sick with worry.

His eyelids fluttered as if they might open but didn't.

Her mind spun like a carousel.

Think, Amber. Think.

All of Monty's brothers, even his cousin who also lived on the Powell ranch, were law enforcement. Any one of them would know exactly what to do and would protect Monty with his life. She took her phone from her purse, but she only had one of their cell phone numbers.

She dialed Logan, thankful he'd given her his number at her father's funeral. He was with the Wyoming State Attorney General's Office, Division of Criminal Investigation. She only prayed she'd catch him before he left Laramie to get on the road to Cheyenne, where he worked.

The line rang four times before he answered. "Powell."

"This is Amber." Her voice broke as she stared at Pandora's lifeless body again. "Where are you?"

Never in a million years had she thought she'd ever call him—the one Powell who had always been in love with her and would've married her in a heartbeat, happily, proudly, if she had felt the same.

"Leaving Divine Treats." Keys jangled over the line. "I had to satisfy my sweet tooth. I'm happy to hear from you. Finally."

The Divine Treats bakery was within easy walking distance, three blocks away. "I need you."

"What is it?" His voice tightened. "What's wrong?"

"It's Monty. You have to come, quickly."

"Did something happen to him? Where are you?"

"At Pandora Frye's." She rattled off the address. "Monty is out. I can't get him to wake up." Her voice was shaky, and she took a steadying breath to control it. "But Pandora…" Hot bile rose in her throat. "There's blood and a knife."

"Is she alive?"

Amber shook her head and then realized she had to use her voice. "No. She's dead."

"Are you sure?"

"Yes." Her gaze trained on the lifeless body, and she had to fight the urge to cover the poor woman. "I'm positive. You have to hurry."

"I'm climbing in my truck now. I'll be there in less than two minutes." A beat of silence. "Did you call 911?"

"No." She wasn't sure what to do. The right thing and the best thing might be different in this situation. Not once had she ever broken the law and she wasn't considering doing so now, but when it came to Monty, she never could think straight. One thing was certain. He needed someone on his side out in front of this. "Not yet."

"Okay. We have to hang up," he said, the sound of a car starting in the background. "Then you need to call 911."

But he didn't fully understand what he was about to walk into. What he was about to see. The bloody knife. The alcohol. The drugs. Pandora—naked, slain.

Oh, God. "Logan, the way this looks—"

"Whatever you're staring at will appear far worse if they pull our phone records and piece together the delay in calling 911." Another pause. "We've been on the line for too long already. I'll be there shortly."

Logan disconnected.

Had she made a mistake in phoning his brother first? She hadn't thought about the police looking at phone records. Would her actions make Monty look more guilty?

She only wanted to help, not hurt him.

A rush of mixed emotions battered Amber. She glanced back at Monty and desperately tried to rouse him. Heart pounding in her chest, she flicked another shocked look at Pandora.

No way Monty would've hurt her, much less kill her.

But someone had. Would anyone besides his family, her and Chance believe in his innocence? Half the town loved the Powells. The other half longed for their ruin.

Amber shook off the thought. The who and why behind this didn't matter at the moment. How many would stand beside Monty or stand against him didn't either. The only thing that did matter was proving his innocence and making sure Monty didn't go down for this murder.

She dialed 911.

Chapter Two

Monty opened his eyes to glaring light and closed them again. His head was thick and throbbing, his throat dry as cotton. A bad taste was in his mouth.

"Mr. Powell! Can you open your eyes?" a strange male voice asked.

Pain thundered through his skull. Something was wrong. If only he could think.

Where was he? Why was someone shaking him? And shouting his name?

At least he was sitting up. Groaning, he forced his eyes open.

The room spun. Music played in the background. His breathing was strained to the point of wheezing. His fuzzy gaze veered past the stranger in front of him and locked onto Amber. She was blurry and then the sight of her cleared up. "What's going on?" he said, his voice low, his throat raw and scratchy.

Was she real? Was he dreaming?

"It's going to be okay, Monty." A warm, gentle palm pressed to his cheek. "You didn't do it. You couldn't have killed her."

Someone was dead.

None of the words coming from her made a lick of sense. "Killed…w-who?"

He was exhausted, like his brain and body were wading through sludge.

"Ma'am, we've already told you to step away from the suspect and to go back into the hall," a stern voice said.

Suspect. He refocused on the man in front of him. A police officer. Laramie PD.

"W-what's happening?" Monty asked, trying to piece things together. But his memories were jumbled.

"Get your hands off me!" Logan's voice was sharp, but his brother was out of sight. "Can't you see he needs help? At least let the EMT check him out."

"Sir, can you look at me?" a woman asked.

He was so thirsty. "Water."

"They need to take him to the hospital," Logan demanded.

The woman knelt in front of him. An EMT. She shone a penlight in his eyes, making him squint.

It felt like a jackhammer chiseled away in his head. "I need water."

"In a minute, sir." She lifted a gloved hand in front of his face, raising her index finger. "Please follow my finger." She moved it to the right and he dropped his head. "Do you know what day it is?"

He struggled to keep his eyes open, to come up with an answer. "S-Saturday? No. Friday. I think."

"What's the month?"

"December."

The EMT pressed something to his mouth. "I need you to blow, sir," she said, and Monty did his best until a strong wheeze forced him to stop. She slipped something on his arm that tightened. A blood pressure cuff. Once she finished, the EMT stepped aside. "He's not drunk. Blood alcohol level is zero. But his blood pressure is quite low and he appears to be having an allergic reaction to whatever drugs he took."

"No drugs," Monty said with a harsh wheeze. He'd never done drugs once in his life.

"He's not in anaphylactic shock and could be hauled in, but we'd advise against it. We should take him to the hospital to be examined," the EMT said.

"If he passes out in a holding cell or worse," Logan said, "it'll be on you. Do you want to risk suspension? Or losing your badge?"

"I'll take the chance to make sure a *Powell* doesn't wiggle out of this one," a cop said. "He's practically been caught red-handed, but your family has a lot of influence."

"He didn't do this." Amber's voice carried from the hall.

The other officer grabbed Monty by the arm and tugged him up, but he wasn't sure he could stand.

Monty swayed on his feet. His arms were wrenched at his lower back and cold cuffs were slapped on his wrists, the sound of metal ratcheting in his ears.

His blurry gaze drifted, landing on a pale body lying on the floor. A nude woman. Pandora Frye.

Dead.

Disbelief and confusion twisted together, spiraling and spreading in his brain.

"It's freezing outside." Amber rushed back into the room. "He needs shoes and a jacket."

One of the officers raised a palm, stopping her. "His clothes are evidence."

"Give him a minute," Logan said from the hall. "He can wear my boots. I can help him put them on."

The officer holding his arm in a vise grip yanked him forward. Monty took two steps. Swirling lights danced in front of his eyes. Then his legs gave out as everything faded to black.

10:35 a.m.

Voices murmured nearby.

Amber?

Confusion fogged Monty's brain. Was he dreaming?

His throat ached as his eyelids slowly lifted. The fluorescent light overhead was painfully bright, blinding him for a moment. His thoughts scrambled like eggs in a sizzling hot pan.

The room came into focus. He was wearing a medical gown, lying in a hospital bed with several instruments attached to him, including an IV. A machine beeped nearby.

Amber hovered close to his bedside.

"You're real," Monty rasped. Jerking fully awake, he tried to sit up but winced when pain cut into his wrists and metal clanged.

"Take it easy." She put a palm on his chest.

His head pounded so hard he thought he might throw up. Closing his eyes and swallowing, he concentrated on breathing to help the dizziness pass.

"Do you want some water?" a familiar voice asked.

He turned his head to see Logan on the other side of the bed. His brother had been in his dream, too. With Amber. No, not a dream. A nightmare. "Yeah."

Logan grabbed a cup from a table and put the straw to his lips. "You're looking much better."

Better than what?

Monty drank, taking long, hard gulps, draining the cup of water.

"You're not wheezing anymore either," Amber said.

His gaze dropped to the metal bracelet on his wrist. "Why am I handcuffed? What am I doing in the hospital?" Taking another steady breath, he tried to calm his raging heart. He stared into Amber's hazel eyes and then at Logan's worried face. "What happened to me?"

The room door creaked opened. Both Amber and Logan shifted focus away from him in unison and moved closer to the bed, bodyguards shielding him from whatever was coming.

Hannah Delaney walked in. She was the fiancée of his cousin, Matt Granger.

Logan visibly relaxed. "They put you on the case?"

"What case?" Monty asked. "Would someone please tell me what's going on?"

Furtive glances were exchanged.

"Monty." Hannah stepped closer. She was petite, blonde and deceptively pretty, like a Disney princess but also tough as nails and capable of taking down a guy twice her size. Only a fool would underestimate her. "You should know I'm here in an official capacity."

Official. She was a detective. Worked mostly homicides.

"I'm assigned to the case for now," Hannah continued. "I could be pulled due to conflict of interest, but if I'm not, I won't be working this alone. Waylon Wright was put on it, too. He *asked* me to leave the scene and to come here." Her tone was sharp, and Monty gathered that she'd been kicked out. "He'll be here shortly."

Monty groaned. There was no love lost between him and the egotistical, caustic detective. They'd had an altercation as teens. Over the years, the animosity had only festered.

Hannah folded her arms. "Anything you say, I'll have to report."

"Then he has nothing to say until his lawyer gets here," Amber said.

Monty shook his head, trying to clear out the fog. "But I don't have a lawyer."

Amber took his hand. Her fingers wrapped tight around his. "Chance is on the way."

"But he's not a criminal lawyer," Logan whispered.

Amber pressed her lips into a tight line. "Chance will do until we can get the best attorney for this kind of thing."

"Explain what's happening." Monty squeezed Amber's hand.

"I found you at Pandora's place." Amber hesitated, swallowed hard. "She's dead. You were unconscious at first. Had difficulty breathing and a rash. They brought you here."

The words awakened a memory. Pandora on the floor. Pale. Still. Blood.

Not a dream or a nightmare.

A shudder ran through him.

"Turns out you were drugged," Logan said. "They're not sure with what yet. They're running tests, but whatever it was you had a bad allergic reaction. The doctor says you got lucky you didn't go into anaphylactic shock. They've had you on an IV drip of meds to counteract it. Your breathing is better. The rash is gone."

"I was at Pandora's," Monty said in a low voice, a statement, not a question, but everything was still cloudy. "But how? Why? What happened?"

Hannah eased closer to the foot of the bed. "You really can't remember?"

He shook his head, ready to expound.

Amber slid her hand over his lips. "That's enough. We need to wait for Chance to get here."

"You should be careful what you say." Hannah's face was neutral, her voice grim. "You're as good as family to me, but I will do my job." She looked over at Amber. "What were you doing at Pandora's this morning?"

Amber opened her mouth as if to answer but then pursed her lips tight.

"I can't help if I don't know." Hannah slid her gaze to Logan. "What were either of you doing there? Do you have any idea how this will look to Waylon?"

"Yes, I do." Logan sighed. "Are you here to help or to do your job?"

"Hopefully, both," Hannah said. "If you believe Monty is innocent and neither of you did anything wrong while at Pandora's, then you've got to talk to me."

Why had they been there?

An ugly thought crossed his mind. What if they had done something wrong, tampered with the crime scene, to help him?

But he shook off the idea. Logan was a sworn officer. His brother would never compromise his integrity. Not even for him.

At least Monty didn't think he would.

A woman wearing scrubs strode into the room. "You're awake. That's good." She checked his IV bag. "I'm Nurse Shelby. How are you feeling, Mr. Powell?"

"Like I've run a marathon, slept for days and still need more rest. And my head is pounding like it's going to split in two. Everything is foggy. I'm having trouble remembering."

"The doctor thinks you were dosed with a date rape drug and a boatload of it, too. We'll know for sure as soon as your blood work comes back." Nurse Shelby took his vitals. "But the mixture of the antihistamines and cortisone with whatever else is in your system is probably amplifying the drowsiness. Don't worry, it'll pass."

"How long until he can remember?" Hannah asked.

"Things will come back to him in a few hours, but he'll never recall what happened while he was blacked out if it was one of the drugs that we suspect."

Logan turned to the nurse. "Does the doctor think it was GHB?"

The nurse shrugged. "Could be. It's one of the most common date rape drugs right along with Rohypnol and ketamine."

But who had drugged him? And why?

"Monty, will you consent to have your medical record released to us?" Hannah asked.

Amber stiffened, tightening her grip on his hand. "Chance can advise us on what to do. If I had thought to call him sooner, he'd already be here. It's still hard to believe that you even need a lawyer."

"I only ask because based on what I've heard I think it will help," Hannah said. "Not hurt you."

Logan nodded. "I agree. I think it'll be the fastest way to get you out of these cuffs." His brother glanced down at the restraints on his wrists.

"Actually, I can take care of that now." Hannah took a handcuff key from her pocket and unshackled him.

"We told the officer who accompanied him here that he shouldn't be restrained in his condition," the nurse said.

"O'Brien." Logan huffed. "The man wouldn't listen to reason because he wants Monty to be guilty. End of story. Forget about due process."

"I'm sorry you went through that." Hannah frowned. "But there are quite a few on the force who'll feel that way simply because you're a Powell."

Monty rubbed his wrists. "Waylon will be one of them."

"No red flags in his record that I'm aware of," Hannah said. "He usually acts first and asks questions later, but a salt-of-the-earth straight shooter. I've known him to be a fair guy."

Logan swore. "Not when it comes to my brother."

Hannah's brow furrowed. "If they keep me on this, I'll make sure everything is handled aboveboard. The medical release?" she asked again.

"Okay." Monty rested back in bed. "If you think it'll help."

"I can see to it for you." Nurse Shelby headed for the door.

"Have it sent directly to the chief of police, Wilhelmina Nelson, as soon as possible," Hannah said.

"Sure. I'll do it right now." The nurse left the room.

Monty looked at his soon-to-be cousin-in-law. "Hey, Hannah. I want you to know, as family and as a detective, that I don't know what happened to Pandora, but I'm sure I didn't kill her."

"Not another word to the police," Amber whispered fiercely and then eyed Hannah with caution.

Everything he'd been told sounded bad. His hazy recollection of Pandora's studio, her dead on the floor, him incoherent, looked even worse. He simply needed Hannah to know that he wasn't guilty of something so heinous. Amber didn't understand how close he was to Hannah. His cousin Matt had been raised alongside him, like a brother, and Amber was aware he considered him as such. But that also meant Hannah was practically the sister he'd never had.

"You should listen to her." Hannah studied his face, her expression one of genuine concern. "If Matt were in your position, I'd advise the same."

He looked up at Amber—his pretty, sweet, fiery Tinker—grateful she was here with him. He'd spent thousands of sleepless nights aching to apologize for the way he'd treated her all those years back. Beg her forgiveness. The worst part, what he regretted most, was making love to her without telling her the truth first—that he'd intended for it to be a marriage of convenience for the land.

During their time together as a couple, everything had changed for him. He'd fallen for her so deeply, so unimaginably hard, he'd wanted forever with her. But when she found out his initial reasons for going after her, it had broken her heart and she'd run from him, from her family, from Wyoming. And it had crushed him.

At her father's funeral, he'd tried to voice the emotions slamming through him. For a moment, they'd gotten close, the clumsy words on the tip of his tongue, but her anger had turned into a different kind of heat, and he'd messed it all up by falling into bed with her instead. Seeing her, touching her, tasting her again was a gut-wrenching reminder of the grave error he'd made. Then she refused to see him anymore and stopped taking his calls.

He would've given anything for a chance to explain. Even though there wasn't any good justification for his actions. But he'd grown up since then. Not a day went by that he didn't hate himself for hurting her. Watching his younger brothers Holden Sawyer and Matt fall in love, with two of them now married and starting families—while he lived alone in the house he was supposed to share with Amber—had forced him to reassess his own empty life, opened his eyes to the fact that the only way to fill the gaping void plaguing him was to win Amber back.

But he'd never imagined that under such dire circumstances, where he might appear guilty of murder, she would support him rather than spit nails at him. A true testament to her character.

The nurse returned, coming into the room carrying a tablet. "I sent what we have so far over to the chief and made a note to have the results forwarded as soon as they're in." She handed Monty the electronic device. "Just need you to sign two forms. Also, there's someone at the nurses' station looking for you. Tall, commanding voice, ruggedly handsome and a rather abrasive man with a badge."

"That'd be Waylon." Monty finished signing the forms and returned the tablet.

"I think I'll leave before he gets in here." Nurse Shelby hurried out of the room.

"What's the deal between you two?" Hannah asked. "And how far back does it go?"

Monty glanced up at the ceiling. "Started in high school and never ended." It was too complicated to say more than that in the time they had.

The door swung open.

Waylon Wright strode in with all the swagger of a man on a mission, sucking the oxygen from the room.

Chapter Three

Waylon shoved into the hospital room and clenched his jaw at the sight of Monty Powell, propped up in a hospital bed, playing the part of the victim when first glance of the damning crime scene made him look guilty as sin.

He tipped his Cutter-style hat to Amber Reyes, glossed over Logan Powell and briefly shifted his gaze to Detective Delaney. If common sense prevailed, she would be removed from the case post haste. But he wasn't going to hold his breath waiting for that to happen. In all likelihood, favoritism would continue to be showered on the powerful, wealthy Powells.

"I believe introductions are unnecessary," Waylon said, "so, let's cut to the chase, Monty. Yeah, you're a Powell and you also happen to be law enforcement." The latter Waylon respected, provided the cop was clean, but the influence and presence of the Powells was ubiquitous. They had enough money to buy senators and governors. Their spawn had infiltrated every corner of law enforcement. Monty was a state trooper. Logan was with the Wyoming Division of Criminal Investigation. Holden was the chief deputy of the sheriff's department. Sawyer was a fire marshal. Matt Granger—their cousin who they treated more like a brother—was the chief of the campus police at SWU, Southeastern Wyoming University. And the youngest, Jackson, was a US marshal in another state. Always craving more power, their mother, Holly, had been recently elected mayor. It was enough to make Waylon raise an eyebrow and wonder at their motives, if it wasn't the desire for control. Unfortunately for them, Waylon wasn't the kind of man who could be bought or easily swayed. "But I have no intention of doing you any favors in this investigation."

"Wouldn't expect you to," Monty said.

Waylon glanced down at his unrestrained wrists. Apparently, the favors had already started. He came to stand at the foot of the bed and eyed Delaney. "Why isn't he handcuffed?"

"The medical staff advised Officer O'Brien when he was brought in that he shouldn't be restrained in his current condition."

"Which at the moment is conscious," Waylon pointed out, "able to speak and quite possibly capable of running."

Delaney scoffed. "Give me a break. He's not going anywhere, and I was present the entire time they were off."

Waylon nudged the brim of his hat up with a knuckle and put a hand on his hip. "Is he a murder suspect?"

"I thought you were going to cut to it," Delaney said flatly, her face deadpan.

"Treat him as such. If you weren't sleeping with his cousin, he'd be in cuffs." When she narrowed her eyes and opened her mouth to respond, he raised a palm stopping her. "A woman is dead, throat slit practically from ear to ear. That man," he said, pointing at Monty while staying laser-focused on Delaney, "was at the scene of the crime, is our only suspect in the homicide, and his prints are on the murder weapon."

Amber Reyes gasped. Concern flooded Logan's face.

But there was only confusion in Monty's expression as he shook his head. "That can't be—"

"Say nothing," Amber said in a harsh whisper, cutting him off.

"I didn't know the prints came back already." Delaney lowered her gaze. "Listen, the cuffs were hurting him and like I said, I was here, watching him the entire time."

"I need everyone to leave the room." Waylon pivoted on his bootheel and glanced between Logan and Amber, but he also meant for Delaney to step outside, too. "I have some questions for the *suspect*."

Amber put a protective hand on Monty's shoulder. "Not without his lawyer present," she said, her voice tart, her cheeks reddening.

"Am I under arrest?" Monty asked, quietly.

"No," Waylon said, wishing that wasn't the case. "Not yet." As much as he'd love to see Monty behind bars, paying the price for any of his wrongdoings, his main concern was getting justice for the victim. Unfortunately, more than a few troubling elements to the case made him question whether Monty had actually committed this crime. It was by no means open-and-shut. He needed all his ducks in a nice, neat row before arresting a member of the Powell family. Especially the heir apparent. "But it doesn't look good for you."

"Looks can be deceiving," Chance Reyes said, sweeping into the room, wearing a crisp power suit and confidence like armor. "I'm Monty's attorney and this conversation is finished." He set down winter clothes and a pair of boots he'd been carrying, presumably for Monty.

"I'm only getting started." Waylon crossed his arms over his chest, irked that they were already preparing to get him out of the hospital. "I have questions for your client that need answering."

Chance plastered on a smug smile. "According to his doctor, it'll be hours before the effects of whatever he was drugged with will wear off completely and his memory will be restored.

She suspects some kind of date rape drug. The results should be in this afternoon."

If that were true, it would take quite a lot to knock out a guy Monty's size. But what reason would Pandora Frye have for drugging him?

"There are still a few questions that he's capable of answering right now," Waylon said. "Such as his whereabouts last night before he went to Ms. Frye's residence."

Chance stood beside his sister. "Is my client under arrest?"

Waylon shook his head. "No."

"Is he being taken into custody?" Chance asked.

They could only hold him for seventy-two hours. Then they'd have to charge and arraign him or release him. Based on everything they had so far, the district attorney would only insist on cutting him loose.

"Not at the moment," Waylon said, but he was a patient guy.

"Then this conversation is done because I'm advising Mr. Powell not to answer any questions and to exercise his right to remain silent."

"Let's make it official." Waylon redirected his gaze to Monty. "Are you willing to answer any of my questions at this time?"

Monty shook his head. "I invoke my right to remain silent."

"Satisfied?" Chance asked. "As soon as he is medically able to be released, he'll be at home."

"Don't try to leave town." Waylon turned for the door. "You'll be under surveillance."

"The heads-up is appreciated," Monty said. "Unexpectedly gracious of you."

"Grace has got nothing to do with it." Waylon flicked a glance at the other detective. "You'd know anyhow." And there was more than one way to get off a ranch that was thousands of acres without being seen by one cop parked at the front gate.

In all honesty, the measure was simply procedural. "Delaney, a word in the hall."

Waylon stepped out of the room and waited for her. He had questions for Amber Reyes and Logan, too. An officer at the scene of the crime had stated that both parties had been present when the authorities arrived and made things difficult.

With Chance present, Amber already acting cagey, Logan being tightlipped and not knowing if Delaney had already helped them get their stories straight, he figured it best to catch them off guard separately without a lawyer around. Sooner rather than later he'd find out exactly why they had been at Pandora Frye's home and no attorney was going to shut down the conversation.

Delaney joined him in the hall and looked him in the eye, shoulders squared and hands clenched at her sides like she was ready for a fist fight. "Do you have more griping to do over the removal of the handcuffs?"

"No. I want you off this case."

Delaney reeled back. "Why?"

"It's obvious, isn't it. You can't be impartial."

"The same could be said of you. I heard about the bad blood between you and the suspect."

He shrugged. "Grievances of teenagers. Nothing more to it than that," he said lightly, trying to dismiss it.

"Felt like a lot more in there to me. You were practically radiating rancor."

"Then you got your wires crossed. Sure, I don't like him, but I don't have to. What happened is ancient history unlike your current romantic relationship with a relative of the suspect. In fact, don't you live on the Shooting Star Ranch, making you a tenant of his parents?"

Her chin rose at that. "The house I live in with Matt and the land it's on belongs to him. I'm not the tenant of any Powell."

"Did he buy it from his aunt and uncle or was it given to him?"

"That's irrelevant and has no bearing on whether or not I should be working this case," she said, not answering the question, which told him everything he needed to know.

"Then you're not only lying to me, but also to yourself."

"Matt's property is legally separate and considered the Little Shooting Star. Some of the income from his ranch goes to the family. But it's his choice. He's under no financial obligation to do so."

"Still sounds like a relevant conflict of interest."

"The decision isn't your call to make. It's up to the chief."

His cell phone rang. He took it from his pocket and glanced at the caller ID. "Speak of the devil."

"Mind if I'm a part of the call?" Delaney asked.

Waylon didn't care. Whatever he had to say to the chief he could say in front of her. He answered, "Wright. I'm with Delaney. Putting you on speaker, Chief."

"Good to catch you both together."

"Speaking of together," Waylon said. "I believe it's best if I work this case alone or with another detective for reasons that you're already aware of, but I'm happy to list them in writing if necessary."

Delaney appeared unfazed.

"That won't be necessary," Chief Nelson said. "This case is rightfully hers. She was the first detective able to respond. I also assigned you to alleviate any possible concerns regarding impartiality. As for a conflict of interest, I believe she's far enough removed from the suspect to do her job and see justice served."

Waylon let a bitter chuckle slip out. "I'm not surprised you think that, Chief."

"What is that supposed to mean?" Nelson snapped.

His laughter curdled in his throat as he realized, though

his comment was rooted in fact, he had overstepped with a superior officer.

The truth was the chief had almost as much reason to give the Powells preferential treatment as Delaney. Chief Nelson was married to the sheriff. The sheriff's sister was Holden Powell's wife. To muddy the waters further, Logan had assisted Wilhelmina Nelson with cleaning up the LPD, cracking a huge case wide open and cementing her as the police chief. Forget about six degrees of separation. In this small town, when it came to the Powell clan, it was more like two.

"One might say you have a possible conflict of interest as well, ma'am," Waylon admitted.

"One might, but are you saying it?"

Waylon met Delaney's prying gaze "I am. Not only are you family for all intents and purposes, but your boss, the mayor, is also the suspect's mother."

Chief Nelson cleared her throat. "I notified Mayor Powell of the situation and informed her that I'll report directly to the governor regarding this case. She emphatically agreed and then assured me that she would in no way meddle in how this was investigated. In fact, she stated that she wouldn't even go to the hospital to check in on her son because she didn't want her presence to be a distraction. I handpicked you to be the lead detective on this homicide because your reputation is above reproach and your character is unimpeachable. So I'm going to let your comment slide. Just this once. Do we understand one another?"

He clenched his jaw at the hint of a grin on Delaney's face. "We do."

"Now that all that's settled, I'm aware the suspect's fingerprints are on the knife found at the scene of the crime. But the medical examiner gave us an estimated time of death between four and seven in the morning. According to Monty's medical record, it doesn't seem that he would have been in any condition to commit the murder. He couldn't even stand up when the EMTs evaluated him."

"Another theory is he was faking it," Waylon said. "Or perhaps he killed the victim first and then took whatever drug he was strung out on."

Delaney raised an eyebrow. "Well, he didn't fake a full-blown allergic reaction."

"This is such a high-profile case I ran it by Assistant District Attorney Merritt," Chief Nelson said. "She believes the DA won't touch this case with a ten-foot pole based on what we have so far. Once his blood work comes in and we know more, we'll reevaluate."

"Speaking of which, how do you have his medical file so fast?" Waylon asked. "The warrant hasn't even been signed yet."

"I asked the suspect to release them to us," Delaney said.

Only because she thought it would help him look less guilty. And so far, it had.

"The warrant just came through," the chief said. "I called the judge and asked him to expedite it."

Now, that was surprising, and also reassuring to see the chief doing everything possible to handle this properly. With the one exception of keeping Delaney assigned.

"I noticed a security camera mounted outside above the door of the victim's residence," Delaney said. "But I wasn't given a chance to see if there was any footage."

She referred to him booting her from the crime scene.

He'd made the right choice and would make it again given the chance. "We'll have to crack her password to access her main hub, but the camera had a micro SD card. Forensics happened to have a card reader. Everything had been deleted except for footage of the night prior showing Montgomery Powell parking beside her and entering the residence along with Pandora Frye at ten thirty. Then nothing else until Amber

Reyes arrived the next morning at seven forty-eight. Followed by Logan Powell at seven fifty-two. Then the ambulance and squad car shortly thereafter."

"Odd that everything else was deleted," Delaney said.

His thoughts exactly. "I figure the victim might've had it set to automatically back up to cloud storage. If so, we'll have access to the entire history in a day or two."

"On the footage, what was the dynamic between Pandora and Monty?" Delaney asked.

"She was smiling, excited, chatted almost nonstop while she unlocked the door. Monty on the other hand didn't look too pleased to be there, but he followed her inside. The camera on the front door was missing a micro SD card."

"Get access to the cloud storage as quickly as possible," the chief said. "And, Waylon, if you have any future concerns of corruption, malfeasance or whatever doesn't smell right to you, feel free to file a report with Internal Affairs in Cheyenne. Otherwise, no more crying about who your partner is. Get the job done and keep me updated. Are we clear?"

"Crystal."

The chief hung up.

He slipped his phone back in his pocket. "We may be partners on this, but I outrank you."

"That you do, Detective *Lieutenant*. Planning to pull rank?"

A detective lieutenant wasn't typical in a large city, but with smaller departments such as theirs, not only was he senior in the investigations division, but he also needed to remain hands-on. He found it easier and simpler to be referred to as a detective while working cases and dealing with others in the division unless circumstances required him to throw his weight around.

"Not at all." Delaney was an excellent cop but had a reputation for not working well with others and a habit of going rogue. It was the only reason she hadn't been promoted a long time ago. "I only bring it up because I don't want you to give me a reason to feel like I have to. That means no coloring outside the lines. You do this by the book, work it with me, every step of the way. If Monty or anyone in that family says a single word to incriminate him or another Powell, you've got to keep me in the loop."

She hesitated for a moment.

A moment too long for his liking. "Don't forget the oath you swore. Your loyalty has to be to the badge." Waylon blew out a heavy breath. "Or you should get out of my way, do the right thing by passing on this one."

"I'm clear on my loyalties."

No doubt she was, but since she neglected to clarify, he still wasn't clear on whether her loyalty was to the Laramie Police Department or to the Powells.

"The last thing I need is an IA investigation into my conduct," she added. "They'll go through my entire history with the department and I don't need that kind of headache."

True. IA would love nothing more than to dig into her file. They'd have a field day.

Delaney straightened her shoulders. "I'll do it by the book. If I learn anything incriminating, you'll know."

He wanted to believe her. Only time would tell.

Waylon nodded and started down the hall. "Pandora Frye's parents need to be notified. Let's find out who they are and see what they have to say."

"In the spirit of an honest partnership, I need to tell you something about her parents and some land she recently inherited. This is much bigger and complicated than you realize because it gives Monty a motive. Not just him, but most of the Powells."

"Sharing is caring." Waylon couldn't wait to hear this. Maybe Delaney would prove to be more a help than a hindrance. "I'm all ears."

Chapter Four

The cell phone on her desk rang. Valentina's heart leaped with expectation at seeing the name of her enforcer whom she'd made a lieutenant on the caller ID. "Please tell me it's done, and that SOB is in jail."

"There's been a problem," Roman said. "He's in the hospital."

"I don't understand." Valentina glanced at her Rolex. "The ketamine would have worn off by the time he was arrested. He should've appeared hungover but alert."

"I had to call the police sooner than intended. I watched them carry him out, handcuffed to a stretcher, and load him into an ambulance shortly after eight."

Eight! Her chest constricted. "That was way ahead of schedule. Why would you do that? What happened?"

"Not what. Who. Amber Reyes happened. She messed up everything."

Valentina sucked in a calming breath. "Explain."

"The Reyes woman showed up more than two hours early, throwing off the timing of things," Roman said. "I had gotten out of there just before she arrived. It's a good thing I spotted her before I left. At least I called 911 right after she went inside. I'm fairly certain I made the call before she did, *if she did*, but I'm not sure if the plan will still work."

Valentina restrained impulsive words of aggravation. "You assured me you had things under control."

"And I did. Until Reyes decided to ignore the time set in the text message that I had Pandora send to her. She also must have called one of the brothers because Logan Powell showed up there, too."

So many brothers and a cousin to boot. "Remind me, which one is Logan? Is he the fire marshal?" She knew that Holden was the sheriff's deputy but couldn't keep track of the rest.

"No, that's Sawyer. Logan is with DCI."

Valentina rolled her eyes. How was it possible for them to all be in law enforcement? "Did you take pictures of everything? Time stamps on their arrival?"

"Of course. Never know if we could use something later."

She shoved back from behind her desk and paced in the office that was once her beloved father's. "This could work to our advantage. Maybe Amber Reyes and Logan Powell might have done something stupid in an effort to help Montgomery." If anyone knew how to tamper with a crime scene, it was a cop. If so, then things would work out even better than she had originally hoped. She would not only take him down, but his law enforcement brother and former fiancée, too.

"If they tried, they wouldn't have had long," Roman said. "The police were on the scene only moments after Logan stepped foot inside. Not enough time to dispose of evidence that would point to Monty. Only enough rope to hang themselves."

"Their presence will be incriminating once the detective on the case finds out they were there before the authorities, especially if you were the only one to call 911. It'll beg the question of whether they corrupted the crime scene. Do you know who's assigned to the case?"

"I do. You won't like it."

She was never one to be coddled, not even as a child. Always ready to have the Band-Aid ripped off no matter how much it would hurt. "Tell me."

"Hannah Delaney was first on the scene and they're leaving her on the case."

Valentina had never heard of the detective. "What am I missing?"

"Delaney recently started a relationship with the cousin. Matt Granger. It's serious. They're engaged. Live together on the family ranch."

Letting out a growl of frustration, she picked up her coffee cup and threw it against the wall, smashing the mug to pieces. For a reckless second, she considered ordering Roman to shoot Montgomery Powell in the head. But then she remembered the promise she'd made to her father—his dying wish for Montgomery to suffer the way her brother had—and stopped herself.

"There is good news," Roman said. "Waylon Wright was made the lead detective. From what I've heard, he hates the Powells. Any shred of evidence that points to Montgomery being guilty, he'll chase it. The man is a bloodhound. Nothing and no one will get in his way."

One small consolation in the face of this unmitigated disaster. "Why did that wretched woman have to show up so early and ruin months of meticulous planning?" Amber Reyes would have to pay.

"It was way too soon for the authorities to find Montgomery. We needed at least another ninety minutes. Possibly two hours. I gave him a precise dose for his body weight. He would've been awake on his own by then. The authorities only would've run a general tox screen to check his blood alcohol content and to see if he did any of the cocaine that I left in the studio, but now they'll order a full panel. They'll find the ketamine in his system."

I should've taken care of it myself.

She dropped down in her chair. Tapping her long fingernails—painted the color of blackened berries—on her desk, she considered the situation. Forced herself to focus on the things going in their favor. "This is simply a hiccup." Concentrating on the positives and how to maximize them was the only way forward. She never wallowed.

"No. This is worse than that. There's more. It's my understanding that he had a reaction to ketamine. I couldn't have known he'd be allergic, but it's still my fault. *Perdóname.*"

Roman—once her father's right-hand man and now hers—made it difficult to remain angry with him. He was fiercely loyal. Took responsibility for his mistakes, which were rare. When they did occur, he always asked for forgiveness.

He was also quite attractive. Slick bald head and a touch of stubble, giving him that rough appeal she found alluring. An excellent lover, too. She'd sampled his goods herself. If only she didn't need him for the dirty work, like seducing Pandora Frye and killing her, she might've given him a place at her side. As her partner. Not as equals, of course. She would remain in charge of her father's empire, as queen, while he could've been her prince consort.

It was lonely at the top. The seat of power was never meant to fall to her. Santiago was supposed to take over the cartel, but with her brother's brutal death, she was the only one left to reign.

Her heart ached. She could use her father's wise counsel now. He would know precisely what to do to avenge Santiago.

All she could do was trust in the plan. And in Roman. The one person she could count on.

"You're taking great risks for me," she said. *For her father. For Santiago.* Far beyond the scope of anyone else in her organization. "Thank you. Now we have to do damage control."

"I don't know how it'll play out," Roman said, "but I don't think they're going to arrest him just yet."

Focus on the endgame. "Whether or not he ends up in jail today matters little." Ultimately, his final destination would be a cell behind bars, where he would watch, helpless to do anything, while she tore apart his family. Only then would he die. While incarcerated. Painfully. Slowly. The way her brother had. "The first seed of doubt has been planted. His character and motives will be questioned. Opportunity, means and motive are clearly there. He won't be allowed to return to his position with the state police unless this is resolved in his favor. This will give us the chance we need for the next step."

"I won't be able to be your eyes and ears at the hospital. I'm not sure when he'll be discharged."

Roman was working on something else equally important for her.

"Never mind that. I'll send Leo to get an update. It'll be easier for him to contact me." Her driver was a capable man, interested in taking on a larger role in the organization.

"I'm sorry. If this murder doesn't stick to him—"

"We can't wait to find out. We need to expedite the rest of the plan. Starting today."

"Move up the timeline on everything?"

"Yes."

"Are you sure that's wise? It could raise unwanted suspicion."

"We have no choice now. Do your part. On my end, I'll get Leo to help me. It'll be the perfect test for him," Valentina said. There was more than one way to make a person suffer. "I've got to go. I need to reach out to our contact inside the highway patrol."

The day after Montgomery hit her family's radar, she'd begun her search for the perfect person to infiltrate the state troopers. One thing her father taught her was to never underestimate the power of an inside man.

"You're going to have the phone planted?" Roman asked.

"Yes. Go handle the remaining things on your end. Don't fail me again." Before he made any promises, she hung up. Then she dialed Officer Nicholas Foley. "It's me. I need to put you in play."

"Yes, ma'am. How may I be of service?"

"The item I sent for you to hold until I gave further instructions," she said, referring to the burner phone, "needs to be found in Montgomery Powell's locker when it's searched." The phone was Roman's suggestion. Once he explained his rationale behind the idea, she'd wholeheartedly agreed that planting the phone at the right time would be genius.

"You're sure it will be searched?" Foley asked.

If the LPD was doing their job, his locker would definitely be searched. She couldn't give any guarantees, but, if necessary, she'd get Nicholas to whisper a suggestion in the right ear. "I'm sure this must be done."

"It might prove difficult."

"You're not being paid double what you're making wearing the badge because you were going to be asked to do something easy. Get it done. Within the hour."

"I'm on patrol. I can't just leave and waltz into the station."

Excuses were number two on her list of things she hated, right after failure. "Figure it out. Quickly. Or I have no further use for you. Or your wife." Both were her employees. Both would suffer the consequences. "Do you understand what I'm saying?"

"Yes, ma'am. I'll see that it's done."

"You had better. For your wife's sake, if not for your own." She hung up and had one of her guards posted near her office fetch Leo.

He knocked twice.

"Come in," she said.

Leo entered, eyeing the broken mug on the floor. "Would you like me to have someone clean it up?"

"No." The maid would take care of it later. She beckoned him forward.

Dressed in his usual simple, off-the-rack, black suit and white shirt with a skinny necktie, he stopped right in front of her desk, hands clasped behind his back like a good little soldier still in the army. He followed orders so well, sometimes she found it hard to believe he had ever been dishonorably discharged.

"Time to get your hands dirty," Valentina said. "Go to Laramie. Montgomery Powell is in the hospital. Send me updates on his status. I want to know when he's released and who his visitors are. Then I need you to put your sniper skills to use." She removed a folder from her top desk drawer and opened it. Sifting through the photos, she found the one she wanted and slid the glossy 4x6 across the desk to him. "This is your target."

His dark eyes widened. "Really? Him?"

She gave a single nod.

"Do you want him injured or—"

"Dead. A bullet to the stomach would be better than the heart." When he raised an eyebrow, she explained. "Nice slow bleed-out over an instant kill shot." *To give loved ones false hope.* "And I'd prefer you to do it in front of Montgomery, if at all possible. They live on a compound. You'll have to get creative. There'd be a sweet bonus in it for the personal touch provided you can pull it off where Montgomery can see it."

Leo grinned. "I'll head out now."

"Max will go with you," she said, deciding on the guard with the hulking chest and goatee to accompany him. Max would keep an eye on Leo and report back on how he handled himself.

Leo picked up the picture and stared at the target. "What have you got against Montgomery Powell, if you don't mind me asking?"

An eye for an eye. She wanted that man to suffer unimaginably. Before he died, he'd feel the same heart-wrenching pain that she had endured. The thought of her brother, beaten and stabbed in jail, and her father's subsequent stroke had her chest constricting again. She had to concentrate to take a simple breath.

"I do mind," she said. "All you need to know is that you begged for this opportunity to prove yourself. Don't waste it."

Leo slid the picture into his pocket. As he opened the office door, her nephew bolted into the room faster than a rocket. He was holding Legos and a piece fell off, clattering to the floor. A harried nanny ran in after him, and Leo left, closing the door.

"Auntie Val, Auntie Val! Look what I made." The four-year-old leaped into her lap.

"Let's see it."

Julian held up the toy.

She scrutinized it for a moment. "Is it a gun?"

"No, silly." He giggled. "It's an airplane."

"Of course, it is, but it's lost a wing." Not her fault he held it like a gun and a piece was missing. "You're so smart and creative." She ruffled his dark curls and hugged him tight. Every time she held her brother's son, she felt a little closer to Santiago.

"I'm sorry, madam." The nanny wrung her hands as her face creased with worry. "He got away from me."

"I was about to take a break anyway. Julian, how about we have lunch together today?"

"Yippee!" He hopped down. "Can we have pizza and carrots?"

"Of course." Valentina closed the file, covering the pictures of the rest of the Powell family and tucked it back in her desk.

One way or another, Montgomery was going to get what was coming to him.

Of that, she would make certain.

Chapter Five

Amber walked through the lobby of the hospital alongside Logan and Monty, who sat in a wheelchair, pushed by Nurse Shelby. Chance had left a couple of hours earlier to go over the case with the top criminal defense attorney in Cheyenne and was planning to meet them at the Shooting Star Ranch for a family meeting.

As they neared the exit, she slowed to a stop. "That vile reporter, Erica Egan, is waiting outside. She even has a camera guy."

"I thought she was bad before," Logan said, "but her promotion to the KLBR TV station has only emboldened her."

"Are they here because of Mr. Powell?" Shelby asked.

"Yeah, they are." Logan's voice sounded tight and annoyed. "No way they've been waiting out there in the cold for hours. Someone must've tipped them off that you were being discharged."

"I can take you to a different exit. Most people don't know about it. We use it for mothers with newborns, so they don't have to encounter as many folks."

"That'd be great," Logan said.

Monty nodded. "Much appreciated."

"It's this way." Shelby turned down a hall on the right.

"I'll use the main exit to distract them," Amber said. Her father's death had been big news in the area. Reporters jumped at the opportunity to remind everyone how close the Powell and Reyes families were. She'd caught her picture in the paper and on TV more than once since she'd been home. "I'll meet you at the house."

"See you soon." Logan flashed her a sad smile. "Thanks for everything."

Down the hall, Monty grumbled, "I'm fine to walk on my own. I don't need a wheelchair."

"Sorry, it's policy," Shelby said. "You're free to do as you please once you leave the hospital."

Amber stood still, giving them time to reach the less frequented exit. Once they disappeared from sight, she headed for the sliding doors.

"Ms. Reyes." Erica Egan rushed toward her, holding up a microphone. Her colleague pointed the camera at Amber. "Were you here at the hospital to see Montgomery Powell?"

Although Amber wanted to run to her vehicle, she forced herself to slow down. "I was here for personal reasons." Over the shoulders of Egan and the cameraman, she spotted Logan and Monty hurrying across the parking lot.

"Would those reasons have anything to do with Mr. Powell?" Egan asked.

"As I've already stated, it was personal."

"What to do you think of Monty Powell being the prime suspect in the murder of Pandora Frye?"

Stopping, she gathered her thoughts. "First, the murder is a horrific tragedy. Second, I believe the evidence will eventually show that Monty is innocent."

"Are you saying he isn't capable of murder?" Egan thrust the mic back in Amber's face.

"Yes, I am."

Logan's truck zipped out of the lot and turned onto the road.

"A source has told me that the two were lovers and this was a crime of passion," Egan said. "How long were they sleeping together?"

Amber's cheeks burned, her chest tightening. All she could do was shake her head at the accusation.

"Would you care to comment, Ms. Reyes?"

"Yes. Get better sources. Please excuse me." Amber pushed past them and hustled toward her Jeep. She dug into her purse, rifling through it for her keys. Why hadn't she simply put them in her pocket?

Finally, she found them. She hit the key fob, unlocking the door, and rushed around the rear to get to the driver's-side door.

"Ms. Reyes." Waylon Wright tipped his hat at her. "I have a couple of quick questions for you."

He'd been waiting to ambush her.

She looked around. No sign of Hannah. "I'm sorry, but I need to go. I'm expected somewhere."

"At the Shooting Star Ranch for a big Powell meeting? I figure they'd be keen to circle the wagons since Monty has been discharged."

She swallowed past the lump in her throat. "I don't have time to talk right now." She reached for the door.

But he stepped in the way, blocking the handle. "This won't take long. Make time. Unless you have something to hide. See, I'm starting to get the sneaking suspicion that you might. Considering how you insisted that Monty not talk to me. An innocent person has nothing to fear."

"Monty is innocent, but I believe he has a great deal to fear from you. As for insisting that he wait for his lawyer before answering questions, it was common sense. He wasn't in a good state of mind since he was under the influence of—"

"Ketamine. Yes, I'm aware. His blood work came back." He pulled out a notepad and pen. "Still doesn't explain your reluctance to answer a few questions yourself. Might that have something to do with the terms of your father's trust?"

She stiffened. "What do you mean?"

"It's simple. The land you stand to inherit has a river running through it. A river that is vital to the Shooting Star Ranch because their cattle depend on it. Your father had a neighborly agreement with the Powells, giving them access to the water until his death. If you don't marry Monty Powell in a little less than a month, then you'd lose everything and Pandora Frye stood to inherit it all. It would explain why he was sleeping with her," Waylon said, and the fire in her cheeks spread to her chest. "As an insurance policy in case things didn't work out with you. But maybe things turned sour last night, giving him a motive to kill her."

Amber shook her head. "The amount of ketamine in his system would've been too high."

"He could've killed her and then taken ketamine."

"Why would he do such a thing?"

"To put reasonable doubt in the mind of a jury." He rested his forearm on her 4x4. "A cop planning a murder would think of that kind of thing."

"Not Monty."

"You seem certain. If he's such a great guy, why haven't you married him? Based on your father's will, I'm sure he'd make an eager husband."

Fiddling with her keys, she averted his keen gaze. "Marriage should be based on love. Not money." But she couldn't squeeze blood from stone. She never wanted any man to feel forced to marry her. "Monty is flawed, but he isn't a murderer."

"For the Powells, that river and your land it's on are priceless. Even if he didn't kill her, it still gives every member of his family a motive. Also gives you a pretty big one, too."

Amber staggered back a step, shocked at the redirection of his line of questioning. "Are you accusing me?"

"Why were you at your half sister's house this morning? And if you even think of stonewalling me, I'll cross this parking lot and give Erica Egan the scoop of her life. She'd gladly swallow every crumb I threw her way, particularly the part about you being at the scene of the crime. This can play out in the court of public opinion if you want."

Egan would paint a story that was thirteen shades of ugly, portraying Monty or even her as a cold-blooded, greedy murderer. Amber sighed, her breath crystallizing in the chilly air. "I assume you know that she also inherited my family home."

Waylon gave a single, slow nod. "I do."

"I wanted her to sell it to me and Chance. She agreed to meet me. To discuss it. She texted me last night, telling me to come over this morning."

"May I see the text?"

He already seemed to know so much. What harm could it do?

She pulled out her phone and brought it up.

Waylon took her cell, glanced at it and scrolled through several other messages. "You've had some heated exchanges back and forth."

Lowering her head, she did her best to tamp down the spurt of anger. "I didn't know I had a half sister until the reading of the will. Not the best way to find out. I just lost my father and I didn't want to lose our family home, too."

"The message told you to come at ten. Why did you arrive so early?"

She huffed out a breath. "It was silly. I've been working as a substitute teacher while I'm in town. School starts at nine. I felt like inconveniencing her rather than be the one inconvenienced."

"Are you involved with Monty?"

Blood drained from her face, her entire body growing heavy as stone. "W-w-we aren't a couple."

The corner of his mouth hitched up. "Have you ever been romantically involved?"

She clenched her fingers around her keys. "Years ago."

"What about since you've been home, after the reading of the will and he learned about the trust?"

Everything inside her went numb. She glanced past him at the door. "This is taking too long. I need to go."

"When you arrived early at your sister's place and discovered that Monty was with her, did it anger you?"

"Half sister." She looked up at him. "If you're asking me whether or not I killed her, I didn't. I swear it. The front door wasn't closed all the way. It swung open after I knocked. She was already dead."

"I believe you," he said, quickly, easily.

Relief crept through her. "You do?"

Waylon nodded. "You got there at seven forty-eight. You didn't kill her. But I think you were worried that Monty had. Why else would you call Logan?"

She grimaced. How did he know that?

"This looks bad," Waylon said. "Your phone call could get Logan into a lot of trouble, legally, professionally, but an honest answer could make it better."

The last thing she wanted was to incriminate Logan in some way or make this worse. "I freaked out." She shrugged. "He popped to mind because I realized he would know what to do."

"What did he tell you?"

She hesitated.

"I only want the truth," he said, his tone comforting and sincere, "and you've got nothing to hide, right?"

"He told me that he was at Divine Treats and would come straight over, but to hang up and call 911."

"Logan told you to call right away *before* he got there?"

She nodded. "He insisted on it."

Waylon handed over her phone.

The screen was on her recent calls. He'd toggled over and had already seen how long they'd spoken and that she'd called the authorities right after. "Were you testing me?"

"I prefer to think of it as poking around to get a good sense of a person." He stepped away from her Jeep. "You never answered my question. Have you been romantically involved with Monty since you've been home?"

This man kept finding ways to corner her and squeeze out answers. "You lied, Detective Wright." She opened her door.

He narrowed his eyes. "That's the first time anyone has ever accused me of lying. About what exactly?"

She climbed inside the Jeep. "You said this wasn't going to take long. Now, I'm late for an important meeting."

"Apologies, ma'am. I stand corrected. And that's twice you've dodged the same question about the nature of your relationship with Monty since the reading of the will. Some might consider that an answer."

Amber closed the door, cranked the engine and peeled out of the lot.

Chapter Six

A hundred different things crawled through Monty's head with his brain still pounding as he rested his eyes during the drive to the ranch. He was grateful for the silence.

In a few minutes there would be nonstop chatter and strategizing.

"We're here," Logan said far too soon.

Monty opened his eyes. "This is a nightmare."

His brother gave a grunt of assent and put the truck in Park.

"Thanks for having my back, looking out for me."

"Always. You're my brother." Logan pressed his lips in a firm line, his jaw tightening.

Clearly, his brother was weighing his words, deciding if he should give voice to them. "Are you going to spit it out or keep it to yourself?"

"Most of what I have to say should probably wait until we're all together."

"And the rest of it, you want to get off your chest now?"

"This isn't about whether you're guilty. I know you didn't kill anyone."

"Thanks. I'm sensing a *but* there."

"But sleeping with Pandora, the fact that Amber had to

see you with her, like that." Logan shook his head. "Her of all people."

"I don't even know why Amber was there, but that's beside the point. I didn't—"

"I'm not finished," Logan said, cutting him off. "You really hurt her bad with the engagement, scheming with Dad and Mom, lying to her the way you did. When are you going to stop being a source of pain for her?" He clenched his hand into a fist. "Enough is enough. I won't stand by and watch you do it again. So help me, I'll knock your head off myself first. Do you hear me?" Logan jumped out, slamming the door closed behind him.

Monty scrubbed a hand over his face, wanting to disregard Logan's anger. After all, Logan was his least favorite brother and that included Matt in that count. Yet, the brutally honest words rang true in his head.

To many, his history with Amber looked black-and-white. Simple. It was anything but.

He stared up at his family home. His parents had meticulously crafted the house. Floor-to-ceiling windows, ten bedrooms, twelve bathrooms, gourmet kitchen, gym, movie room and state-of-the-art automation. They had designed it to entice their children to stay close. They often talked about their legacy, the importance of the ranch, about all the weddings, holiday celebrations and big birthdays they wanted to have here. With plenty of room for grandkids, extended family, in-laws and friends to stay.

More than a home, more than a ranch, this sanctuary embodied their hopes and dreams. And those of many Powells before them who had sacrificed so much in the hope it would be passed to the next generation.

He'd never wanted the responsibility of that legacy. Fought against it for as long and as hard as he could until that fateful day in the kitchen with his folks.

He could still hear his parents like it was yesterday.

"All I've ever wanted was for my sons to take up the mantle," Dad said. *"Do what my father and his father before him has done. Hold tight to the ranch, grow, prosper. I have five boys and a nephew I love like a son. Six of you. I figured at least one of you would surely want to run this place."*

"I can't speak for the others," Monty said. *"I want to be my own man. Make my own choices. Live my own life. Not one you've decreed."* He turned to his mother. *"You claim all you want is for us to be happy."*

"That's true," she said. *"But you seem miserable being a state trooper. Driving around handing out speeding tickets half the time. Like you picked that job just to spite us."*

Monty heaved a breath. *"You're missing the point. I picked it. It was my choice."*

"This land, being a part of the ranch, working with the cattle makes you happy," she said. *"It's what you were born to do. I've seen how you thrive."* She sighed. *"Amber has been in love with you forever and I know that if you open your heart to her, you're bound to fall in love. And unlike most of those fast fillies you usually go after, Amber will stand up to you and not let you treat like her garbage, which is what you need. A woman with a backbone."*

Monty chuckled. He'd pay to see that. The reality was Amber doted on him every chance she got. He could do no wrong in her eyes.

He didn't want a doormat. Even if she was perfect for him, which she wasn't, he still wouldn't want her—a woman picked for him by his parents, a bride he was expected to marry.

Like this ranch that he was expected to love and oversee until the day he died.

No, thank you.

"The two of you are opposite sides of the same coin." Mom took his hands in hers and met his eyes. *"You could have a*

wonderful marriage with Amber. Just give it a chance. Put the work in and really try. You'll see."

Pulling away, he turned his back on her. "No."

"Yes! You, insolent son of a gun!" his father said, his eyes filled with anger and...pain. "I have never asked anything of you. We have never asked. If we don't control that land with the river, anything could happen to it. You don't marry her, the land will go to someone else. A person with no love for our family. Someone who might one day decide to dam it."

"Whoever it is, we could buy from them," Monty said, suggesting a reasonable solution.

"We can't tell you who." His father clenched his jaw. "But trust me. That person won't take our money. Their ears have been poisoned against the idea. They'll sell it, perhaps to someone who wants to build a big, noisy resort. Frightened cattle with no access to water means the end of this ranch. You don't do this, everything we've built will be lost."

Monty grimaced, his heart throbbing like an open wound.

"For once in your spoiled life, you're going to put this family ahead of yourself!" Dad jabbed a finger in his chest. "We need the river and you're the only one who can get it for us. You'll marry that girl. Get yourself a sidepiece if need be."

Mom gasped. "Buck! How dare you. Amber deserves a real husband."

"A cheating husband is still a real one," Dad said.

Monty imagined sex with Amber as vanilla. Boring. She was so young, seven years his junior. He'd never seen her go out with anyone, and she was probably a virgin. He preferred spicy girls with more experience, but he would never humiliate her or any wife by treating her like that. "I'm not the cheating kind."

"Even better." Dad threw his hands up. "We need you to do this, son."

As much as Monty despised the idea, the pressure was un-

relenting, making him consider it. "If I did do this, I'd have to tell her up-front that it's just for convenience only."

"You can't." Mom shook her head, her eyes weary. She looked bone-tired. "Carlos made it very clear. He doesn't want her to know. That's why he's putting things into motion now, long before he dies, and she learns she'll inherit all the land."

Of course, Mr. Reyes wanted this to feel organic for Amber rather than orchestrated. He'd like to give that man a piece of his mind, trying to dictate whom Monty should marry, whom he should love, how he should live. Just as bad and manipulative as his parents.

"Don't tell her. Woo her. Get hitched," Dad said. "Give it a solid go for two years, putting in the work like your mother said. Those are the rules. After that, you can decide about forever and it'll be whatever life you want. Free from the legacy that you're too good to carry on, and may I live long enough to have a grandchild who'll do so."

Monty felt like a block of stone split in two, cracked right down the middle, but keeping the truth from Amber made him sick to his stomach. "No. I won't do it."

A week later his father had a heart attack. At his bedside, his mother begged Monty to agree.

Was it weakness? Fear? Love? Duty? All Monty knew was he'd caved.

He courted Amber and proposed. For the land. For the river. To make everyone, other than himself, happy.

They all thought he'd told Amber some great lie.

But he never said those three little words, *I love you.* Not once. He never painted a rosy picture of happily-ever-after. Never whispered sweet things in her ear. Never wooed her. Never seduced her. He didn't have to do any of that stuff. Plainly asked her out and things went from there. She had been the one to initiate sex. As he'd guessed, she'd been a virgin. He'd underestimated the power of that experience on both sides. To be her first everything—not something he took lightly.

The truth was, he didn't have to put in much effort to get the relationship to bloom. She got caught up in a fantasy of her own making, and he let her.

He let her because it made her happy. He let her because his parents had promised his duty would be done. No more pressure for him to take over the ranch if only he married Amber Reyes. He let her because he reached a point where he believed he could make it work. Make it real. Give her what she needed. Saw she was what he wanted after all. As much as he'd been loath to admit it, his mother had been right about him and Amber. Forced together, a collision of smashing pieces, they fit and became easily entangled.

They had just found their footing as a couple, enjoying the discovery of one another, with him surprisingly excited for the future. A future with her. Instead of feeling he had settled for someone else's choice, he simply felt settled. Delighted by how deeply, madly he'd fallen for her. How she knew him better than he knew himself. Like they were really meant to be.

Then it fell apart. Because he hadn't been honest.

Still, he'd been wrong to do it. After she left, he missed her something awful. A lot more than he ever thought possible. There was a hole in his life, where she had always been. Sometimes he lay awake at night, especially during the past four months—thinking about Amber, about the time they'd spent together, about how right she felt in his arms, about how the sex had been vanilla sweet and spicy hot, the best of both— and he tossed and turned. Sick down in his soul with regret.

Now everyone probably thought history was repeating itself and he'd lured Pandora Frye into some romantic web.

What a fool he'd been to go to her place last night only to talk about a potential deal they could make for the land if Amber didn't marry him. His mountain of mistakes kept growing higher.

He had a sinking feeling that he was playing right into someone's hands. Whoever had killed Pandora was trying to frame him for murder.

But why? Did it have something to do with the Reyes land? The river? Or was there another reason?

Until he had answers, he might have a tough time proving his innocence.

Chapter Seven

By the time she pulled up to the sprawling Shooting Star Ranch, which was really a compound, and waited for the grand wrought iron gate to open, she was fuming.

Where was Hannah? How did Waylon find out the details of the trust so fast? Had Detective Delaney told her new partner?

The main house came into sight with a mesmerizing backdrop of the mountains. A modest term for the massive estate that was a haven of luxury.

A lifetime ago, this had been a place that Amber loved. Not for the amenities or upgrades that the Reyes house lacked. Once, in a dream never meant to be, she'd thought this ranch was going to be home.

She pulled into the circular driveway behind a long line of vehicles. The only two people who wouldn't be at the meeting were Jackson and Sawyer. They'd both come to her father's funeral. It had been nice to catch up with them and to discover Sawyer had married his high school sweetheart, Liz. Theirs was a tragic story but one with a happy ending. It would be nice to see them again in a couple of weeks for Christmas.

The rest of the boys lived on the ranch. Holly and Buck had built Monty a cottage farther back from the main house after he had proposed to her. Meant for the two of them. Holden and his wife had their own cottage now, with a fourteen-month-old son and another baby on the way. The kind of life Amber had once fantasized about having with Monty, being his wife, living on this ranch. Even though her dream had crumbled to ash because of his lie, he'd still decided to move into the house that was supposed to be theirs, where they were going to have a family and raise their children.

Climbing the stone steps of the main house, she put her hand on her belly one last time. Once she walked through those doors, she didn't dare call any attention to the life growing inside her.

She didn't bother to knock. They never locked the front door and already expected her.

"You made it," Buck called out to her as he came down the stairs. At sixty-five with salt-and-pepper hair, he exuded the virility and indomitable strength of a man half his age. After his heart attack, he'd cut back on drinking and stopped eating red meat. He was still handsome in the fit and tailored way of the wealthy. In his arms, he carried his first grandchild, Kayce, and his daughter-in-law was beside him.

Grace was a nurse and the nicest person, caring and thoughtful, making sure that Amber had everything she needed the week of her father's funeral, though they barely knew each other. Since then, she called regularly to check on Amber and invite her to lunch.

Not only was Grace easy to like but also a natural beauty. Flawless brown complexion and sparkling eyes. At eight months pregnant, she glowed, her belly round and tight under the empire waist of her dress, hair falling in long, dark curls around her shoulders. All soft curves and fertility. Somehow, she had only gained weight in her stomach. While Amber was practically subsisting on crackers and already packing on the pounds. But Grace's mother was the famous supermodel Selene Beauvais, which was like hitting the genetic lottery.

"They're in the great room talking now." Grace gave her a warm embrace. The best hugger, too. "Kayce was napping in a guest room and woke up. Buck insisted on coming with me to get him."

"I was so focused on ranching when my own were young that I didn't realize how much I missed until this little fellow was born." Beaming, Buck kissed the boy's forehead. "They grow so fast. I don't want to miss a single minute this time around." He stared into the boy's bright brown eyes. "You're going to grow up to be a rancher like your grandpa. Aren't you? Say yes, yes, I am," he said with a smile for the child in his arms. "As soon as you're old enough to ride, I'm buying you a pony."

"You're going to spoil him," Grace said.

"That's what grandfathers are supposed to do."

Kayce was the perfect mix of Holden and Grace. Tan with curly blond hair and a calm temperament, and he'd slept through the night since he was three months old. Amber had only seen him fussy if he was hungry.

"Do you want to hold him?" Buck offered.

Amber loved holding babies, the way they smelled, how their warmth soothed something in her soul, but with her hormones all over the place today she worried touching Kayce might bring tears to her eyes.

"I wouldn't dare deny you the pleasure," Amber said. "I'll get a chance the next time Grace and I have lunch."

"Which I hope will be soon." Grace took her arm and ushered her deeper into the house. "Since I'm on leave from the hospital until this one comes," she said, rubbing her belly, "I have free time. We better make the most of it while we can."

Smiling, Amber nodded. "With two under two, you're going to have your hands full."

Grace flashed her a weary expression. "That's an understatement."

"Your mom is flying out soon from Los Angeles to help, right?"

Buck and Grace laughed in unison.

"My mom is coming, but it'll be like having a third child to take care of. She can be pretty high maintenance."

"Holly is on it," Buck said. "She's already spoken to Selene and is putting her up in the main house this time. She also hired one of the best night nurses in the area to help you and Holden for the first few weeks."

"Wow." Grace put a hand to her chest. "But they're so expensive. I can manage. Women do it all the time."

Buck clasped her shoulder. "What's the money for, sweetie, if not to make your lives easier. It's a Christmas gift. Please don't tell her I spoiled the surprise, or I'll never hear the end of it."

Grace smiled. "I won't. Promise."

Raised voices carried from the great room around the corner.

"Waylon thinks you were sleeping with Pandora to get your hands on the land," Hannah said.

"It wouldn't be the first time you've done something like that." Logan's voice held a bitter note that Amber knew was on her behalf.

"If you were," Holden said, "we'd understand, but we need to know."

"I wasn't." Monty's tone was sharp. "She's not my type."

"Are you sure you weren't lovers?" Chance asked. "We all know you've compromised your integrity before to do your duty to this family, regardless of the woman not being your type or who got hurt in the end."

Another person on her side.

"I made a mistake with your sister. I regret ever laying a finger on her wit—"

Buck let out a loud, whooping cough, drawing everyone's attention to them as they entered. Silence descended like a foul odor.

Humiliation burned Amber's cheeks as her stomach sank. Taking a seat in a chair on the far side of the room, she avoided eye contact with the others. She slipped off her gloves and coat, wanting to disappear into the furniture. Maybe she shouldn't have come. But Pandora's murder affected both their families and the prime suspect was the father of her unborn child.

Tension hung over the room, finally eased by a tiny squeal of pleasure coming from Kayce as he smacked his grandpa's cheeks.

She dared look up and found Monty staring at her with a mix of sadness and something else she couldn't quite name. Maybe pity. She was pitiable right then after his declaration about her to all of them.

He stood and took a step in her direction when Holly waltzed into the room. Her presence had him shuffling back and sitting down.

His mother came from the opposite hall and entrance, accompanied by her assistant, Eddie Porter, and her campaign manager turned chief of staff, Brianne Mallard—a woman who never stopped managing Holly's public image.

"Why are you all so silent and still?" Holly asked. "What happened?" Her gaze scanned the room, landing on Amber, and the new mayor pursed her lips. "Oh. I see everyone has arrived. What did I miss?"

"We're discussing whether Monty was sleeping with Pandora," Logan said. "Because it definitely looks that way."

Amber's stomach lurched.

"And I've already told them that I wasn't." Monty leaned forward and rested his forearms on his thighs. "But they don't believe me."

"It's understandable if you're reluctant to admit to it. We

just need to be sure." Hannah scooted to the edge of her seat beside Matt. "Waylon is going to look for proof that you're lying about this because it makes the most sense in light of the terms of the Reyes trust."

Staring at the detective, Amber fumed all over again. The woman was a newcomer to this inner circle. She and Matt had been together less than a year. Although they were engaged, she didn't wear a ring, there was no talk of marriage, or a wedding or kids, and it was plain to see that his uncle Buck and aunt Holly didn't know what to make of it. Amber had asked Matt about it once while casually chatting and he'd intimated that he didn't want to *push* the detective and was happy simply living together. Another thing that raised eyebrows in this circle.

No telling where Delaney's loyalties rested. Amber couldn't hold her tongue a second longer. "How did Waylon find out the details of the trust so fast? He knew everything and interrogated me about it in the hospital parking lot. He only stopped short of accusing me of murdering her, too. Did you tell him?"

The full force of everyone's scrutiny swung to the traitor in their midst. "We spoke to Fiona Frye. She's in Arizona, visiting family. We had to inform her about her daughter's murder over the phone." She hung her head like that had been the hardest task in the world. "She's flying back sometime late tomorrow. We'll get an official statement from her in person on Sunday, but she didn't hesitate to accuse this family of murdering her daughter. Because of the land." Hannah turned to Monty. "She claims she has proof that you were sleeping together."

Monty turned pale as a ghost and looked like he'd just been slapped upside the head by one. "That's impossible."

"She said Pandora was seeing someone," Hannah said, "but her daughter couldn't talk about it yet until things were official. Legally. That by the time her mother got back from

Arizona it would be and she'd be able to tell her everything. Apparently, Pandora also gave her a flash drive as insurance."

"What's on the drive?" Monty asked.

Hannah shook her head. "She never looked. Fiona says her desktop computer is thirty years old and doesn't even have a USB port on it, but she's confident it'll prove you two were in a relationship."

"I can dig up dirt on Pandora Frye and her mother," Brianne said, with a spark in her eyes. "Feed it to the press. Change the narrative. Get us control of the story."

A horrified look crossed Holly's face. "We're not talking about an opponent in an election. Fiona is grieving the loss of her only child. We won't get dirty by tarnishing Pandora's reputation. Or hers."

"Not even if it helps Monty?" Eddie pushed his glasses up the bridge of his nose and smoothed back his hair. "And in turn the whole family? Guilt by association is a real thing for the constituents." He was a mild-mannered, soft-spoken man, at Holly's beck and call.

"He's right." Brianne typed away with one hand on her tablet. "We need to think of your public image."

"No," Holly said, with a wag of her finger. "Not another word about it."

Everyone was just going to let Hannah Delaney skate by without answering the question. Cops and lawyers were good at that, but Amber was equally good at catching it. "Did you tell Waylon about the trust?" Amber asked. "Yes or no."

The detective's gaze flashed up, meeting hers. "Yes, I did."

Matt sighed with a shake of his head. "We should go."

"No." Hannah turned, angling toward her fiancé. "I'm not scurrying out the door with my tail between my legs. They need to understand I made the right call."

"Explain it, then," Buck demanded. "Why you'd hand Waylon a motive on a silver platter?"

"Because as soon as we spoke to the mother, he was going to find out anyway. Figured it was better to use it to my advantage. Before I told him, he was certain he wanted me removed from this case and now he's not so sure. If I'm not on it, then I can't pass along information."

"Such as?" Buck handed the baby to Grace and put his hands on his hips.

"The direction the case is headed."

"Go on," Amber said. "We're going to need more than that."

The detective narrowed her eyes. "The warrant was approved. Monty's truck, house, even his locker at work is going to be searched. Tomorrow, once they have enough officers available to handle it. Since he lives here, they'll have access to the whole ranch. Waylon is planning to use that full authority."

Buck pivoted on his heel and glanced over his shoulder. "You got anything to hide, son?"

"No, sir."

Amber huffed a breath. "Don't say anything else."

Monty rubbed his temples like his head still ached. "But I don't have anything to hide."

"This information sharing is a two-way street," Amber said. "Everything we say, she's going to report."

"Is that true?" Buck asked the detective.

But Logan answered, "It is."

The traitor nodded. "Yes, I have to. I'm still a cop working this case and Waylon is the lead on it."

"We can't talk freely. She shouldn't stay." Amber jumped to her feet. The room spun. She reached out for the closest thing to steady herself and sent a lamp crashing to the floor. Stumbling, she headed for a face-plant, but Chance and Monty leaped up and were at her side. They each grabbed hold of one of her arms.

"Are you okay?" Monty asked.

A new twinge in her stomach around her belly button stole

her breath. "Fine." Amber shook her head, trying to ward off the dizziness. "Low blood sugar. I haven't eaten today. Shouldn't have moved so fast."

"How does a piece of lasagna and a glass of wine sound?" Holly asked. "I'm sure you could use a drink after the day you've had."

Her stomach roiled. "Crackers and ginger ale would be perfect."

"You need to hydrate," Chance whispered.

Holly crossed the room, took hold of her arm and shooed the others away. "Let's go to the kitchen. Grace, darling, please join us."

"Matt," Buck snapped.

"I know, sir." Matt rose from the love seat. "Come on," he said to the detective. "We're leaving. Now."

Grace passed the baby to her husband and trailed them to the kitchen, along with Brianne and Eddie.

Holly sat Amber in a chair at the long wooden table near the marble island. "Grace, please make sure she's all right." Holly whispered something to Eddie, who ducked inside the walk-in pantry.

Grace poured a glass of water, handed it to her before the nurse took a seat beside her and proceeded to take her pulse.

Clutching her tablet, Brianne leaned against the wall, looking bored.

"Here you go." Holly took something from Eddie and shoved it in Amber's face.

A plate with a peeled banana.

The smell made Amber gag. "I think I'm going to be sick."

Holly handed the plate back to Eddie. "You're pregnant."

"What?" Amber stared up at her, horrified by the emphatic statement.

"You haven't eaten all day, but the only thing you want is

crackers and ginger ale." Holly glanced at Eddie. "Please get that for her and applesauce and lemon wedges."

Pam, the housekeeper and cook, stopped what she was doing at the stove. "I'll handle it."

"When your mother was pregnant with you and Chance," Holly said, "the doctor told her to try eating bananas to quell the nausea, but the smell of them always made her want to retch."

Amber considered concocting a story as to why she was sick.

"Those wheels are spinning so fast in your head that I can practically see smoke coming from your ears." Holly sat across from her. "You always did wear your heart on your sleeve and your thoughts were easy to read in your face. Please don't insult me by denying the pregnancy."

What would be the point? Soon enough they would all know the truth. "I am," Amber said.

"Congratulations," Grace said softly and covered her hand with a warm palm. "I've known for a while. You threw up at our last few lunches and you're starting to show. I figured that's why you began wearing baggy clothes. But I thought it best to let you tell me when you were ready." Grace cast a scolding glance at her mother-in-law.

Holly cut her gaze from Grace, sliding it back to Amber. "Is the child Monty's?"

Amber stiffened at the invasive question. "This is very personal and I'm not ready to discuss it." Especially around people she didn't know well. Everyone in the Powell household might have been used to Brianne and Eddie's constant presence, but she wasn't.

"You don't have to say another word about it," Grace said, with a reassuring squeeze of her fingers.

"Please excuse us," Holly said to her assistant and campaign manager as if reading Amber's thoughts on her face.

"And, Eddie, call Vera, tell her that since I've been out of the office today for personal reasons, and with me being busy in town all day tomorrow, we'll have to work on Sunday. I'll be in after the eight-thirty church service and will need her in the office by then. I've got so much work to catch up on."

Vera was Holly's secretary. Amber had met her a couple of times. Nice, hardworking lady.

"Sure thing," Eddie said. "Should I tell her to expect you there by ten?"

Holly nodded. Once they were gone, she put her clasped hands on the table. "I don't wish to be indelicate, but in less than thirty days, land that we need will go to Pandora's next living relative. Her mother. If the child is Monty's, when he finds out, he'll insist on marrying you. Why drag this out any longer? Is the baby his?"

Amber was really going to be sick now.

This kind of pressure was one reason she didn't want anyone besides her brother to know the truth. She also didn't want further humiliation. Unrequited love, the duped former fiancée, the man who broke her heart sleeping with her again out of pity, the unplanned pregnancy. It was the plot of some melodramatic movie or a soap opera storyline.

"If I wanted Monty to marry me out of obligation, I could've had him as a husband ten years ago. The entire room heard him say that I was a mistake and that he regrets touching me." Unwelcome tears sprang up, blurring her vision. "Yes, the child is his. But *I* will let him know when I'm ready." Her eyes burned and she closed them. Still, more tears escaped, and she quickly dashed them away. She refused to let Holly think this was a moment of weakness that she could exploit. Opening her eyes, she pinned the formidable older woman with an unwavering stare. "If you tell him or get one of your flunkies to let it slip or try to push me in the slightest, so help me, I'll disappear. *Unmarried.* Unconcerned what happens to the land or the river running through it. And there's no telling when you'll see this baby. Understand?"

"All right. Calm down, dear," Holly said in an easy-breezy tone. "I think we understand each other quite well."

Pam set a tray in front of her with crackers, applesauce, lemon wedges, a can of ginger ale and a glass of ice.

"Thank you," Amber said to Pam. "What's the lemon for?"

"Take a wedge." Holly pointed to the slices. "Sniff it."

She did and the refreshing, citrusy scent immediately tempered her nausea.

"Worked like a charm for your mother. The applesauce helped, too. See if it works for you."

Willing to give anything a try, Amber spooned a little into her mouth and was surprised she wanted more.

"Right after you ran away all those years back, everyone blamed me and Buck, and of course Monty. But it was your father's decision to write that will and trust that started it. Truth be told, this entire mess is really your fault," Holly said.

Amber almost choked on the applesauce. "Is that some kind of sick joke?"

"After your mother died, and with Chance living in a different state, on the road to becoming a bigwig lawyer, your father was worried about you being alone once he passed eventually. He wanted to give you your greatest, deepest desire. *Monty.* So he hatched this twisted scheme with the trust, playing games with hearts, like people were pawns. *For you.*"

"I thought he was only thinking about leaving me the land back then. He'd already written the trust, with Pandora in it?" Amber asked.

Holly nodded. "As soon as he finished and made it legal, he couldn't wait to tell us all about it on the back porch over a glass of whiskey. About Pandora, too, using her as leverage in the trust. Of course, he knew we'd steer Monty toward you," she said. Amber believed it more possible they shoved him toward her. "And it blew up in our faces when you ran away."

It blew up when she overheard Monty admitting to one of his brothers, Sawyer, that he was only marrying her to get the land for his family because she'd one day inherit it. She had been nothing more than an obligation. A chore on his to-do list.

"I thought Carlos might change his mind and rip up the trust," Holly said. "He might've if you had ever married or moved on with someone new."

Goodness knows, she had tried hard to do so, but no man ever measured up to Peter Pan.

"When that baby is born, you'll understand the desire to see him or her happy, to give them what their heart wants," Holly said. "Too bad you didn't love Logan instead, huh?"

It would've made things easier for everyone if she had.

Grace patted her hand. "Finish eating, then you should go home, rest and hydrate. Nurse's orders. Chance can fill you in on the meeting."

Starving, Amber stuffed a cracker in her mouth.

"Yes, rest up." Holly stood. "I'll be expecting you at the Holiday Tree Lighting ceremony tomorrow. It's from noon to six. I need you there by four thirty. We're lighting the tree with fireworks promptly at five. Your father was meant to have the honor of pressing the button. You'll do it in his stead."

A command. Not a request. *Typical.* "You can't seriously be planning to go through with attending the ceremony," Amber said while chewing on a second cracker. "The police are coming to execute the search warrant tomorrow."

"All the more reason for the entire family to be out of the way," Holly said. "Besides, this is a town function that everyone from Laramie to Bison Ridge looks forward to each year. We've expanded the activities—a children's craft center, petting zoo, pop-up holiday markets, live music and food trucks.

It's grown into a big deal. As mayor I've organized everything and it's my duty to be there. The show must go on, my dear." She turned to head out of the kitchen.

"Holly," Amber said. "You won't say anything, not even to Buck?" She wasn't concerned about Grace spilling the beans to Holden. They'd become fast friends, and if Grace had already known Amber was pregnant for weeks, she'd more than proven she could be trusted.

"Your secret is not mine to tell. I won't say anything," Holly said. "We meddled once before and look how that turned out." She glanced up at the ceiling with a faraway look for a moment. "I want to be in the lives of my grandchildren. All of them. The boys, the women they love, the grandbabies and their mothers—that's all that really matters in the end."

"Thank you." Amber truly meant that. Holly Powell could've made it much harder.

"If you need anything," Holly said, "absolutely anything, please don't hesitate to let me know."

Amber nodded, wanting to feel relieved at not having to deal with future pressure from Holly. Instead, dread filled her in anticipation of the moment when she would have to tell Monty the truth.

Chapter Eight

Saturday, December 7
4:40 p.m.

Are you at the ceremony with Amber, yet? I need to speak
to her.

Hoping he'd finally get a reply, Monty sent a third text to Chance.
He stood on the fringe of the crowd, far from his family, sand-
wiched between a Belgian waffle food truck and another sell-
ing doughnuts and warm apple cider. The delectable aroma was
enticing but he wasn't in the mood for sweets or revelry, or to
put on a show of a united front with the rest of the Powell clan,
pretending everything was fine.

Yesterday, the family meeting had turned into an inquisi-
tion. Even Hannah had been under fire when she was only
doing her best to walk a fine line. Being a part of his big, bossy,
overbearing and close-knit family could be a lot for someone
unaccustomed to it. Heck, plenty of times it overwhelmed
him and was part of the reason he spent so much time off the
ranch. He understood the precarious position Matt's fiancée
was in and respected her efforts to help. The rest of the family should have done the same since he was innocent. None of
them needed to compromise their integrity for his sake.

For some reason, the people closest to him doubted him. Not that it had dampened their staunch support of him.

Sure, he'd made plenty of mistakes, chief among them deciding to talk to Pandora on her terms, but the only thing he was guilty of was being a foolish, insensitive jerk to Amber years ago. Downright reprehensible.

I'm a horrible person.

But he was *not* a murderer.

Looking up from his phone, which still hadn't chimed with a reply from Chance, he caught an elderly couple giving him sidelong glances, whispering and pointing at him. A child leaving a food truck line with a loaded waffle piled high with fruit and Nutella waltzed in front of him. Her mother cringed at the sight of Monty and snatched the little girl away, drawing her close, like he posed a serious threat.

Mrs. Sanders from the Ranch and Feed Supply store noticed him and got out of the line for the doughnut food truck. She'd always been kind to everyone. His family had used their store forever, making them not only loyal customers but substantial ones.

He plastered on a soft smile. "Hello, Mrs. Sanders. How's your husband?"

"You should be ashamed of yourself." She pointed an accusatory finger at his face. "What you did to that girl." Mrs. Sanders reeled back with a disgusted expression, drawing attention from passersby. "I can't believe your mother let you show your face here tonight."

Stiffening, he reminded himself that he wasn't guilty, and the truth would come to light. At least, he hoped it would. "For the record, I haven't been charged because I'm innocent."

"Likely story. Or is the real reason because your mama is mayor?" Her voice rose along with the number of onlookers. Some of whom nodded in agreement. "There are kids around here. This is a family-friendly event. Do the rest of us a favor, go back to your ranch and stay there."

Perhaps standing idle in a spot that drew so much foot traffic, with a uniformed officer babysitting him since he was under surveillance, wasn't the wisest idea after his picture had been splashed across the evening and morning news. All day, he'd dealt with much of the same.

His mother had insisted that he be here with the family to help finish setting up and that his attendance during the remainder of the festivities was mandatory. The least he could do since they were here publicly supporting him. It had been a day of walking around feeling like he wore a scarlet letter branded on his forehead.

Shifting his black Cattleman-style hat forward to shield more of his face, he moved on, deciding it best to circulate. Might be the only way to find Amber before she had to go up for the tree lighting. He was sure she'd disappear after she pushed the button.

With the cop following him, Monty strode by a giant, inflatable snow globe, a line for free horse-drawn hay wagon rides around the town center, a decorated drop box for unwrapped presents to donate to local children in need and the largest Christmas light display in the state with more than a hundred individual pieces. Santa, Mrs. Claus and their elves had arrived by firetruck ten minutes ago and were setting up to hear wishes and take photos in the gazebo. A table beside it offered free cookies and hot chocolate—courtesy of the mayor.

This was the biggest Laramie–Bison Ridge Holiday Tree Lighting celebration ever. His mother had transformed downtown into a winter wonderland fit for a postcard.

He looked over at the stage. His mother stood with his father by her side, both smiling as the women's auxiliary choir sang holiday carols. The children's chorus had already performed and the Cowboy Harmony Group, an all-male singing society, was up later.

His mother was in her element, bringing people together, hosting the ceremony, working the crowd, shoring up Powell defenses by trying to garner public support. Managing anything from a staff to a ranch, to finances, to an entire town, came naturally to her. Hard to believe that at one time she'd wanted to be a federal law enforcement officer like her dad and grandfather. She even had a degree in criminal justice. Then Monty's grandfather got sick, and his parents had decided to take over the ranch. Their duty. Their honor.

He stared at his mother, so proud of her.

Being mayor suited Holly Powell, like she was always meant to have the job. In the same way being a rancher suited his father. The Shooting Star had been a part of his family for six generations.

A legacy Monty still didn't want. One of his other brothers was welcome to have it and run the place. Not that being a state trooper fulfilled him. Quite the opposite in fact. Law enforcement was in his DNA on his mother's side, but every time he put on the uniform, he felt like a fraud living the wrong life.

At least it was a life of his own choosing. A man should have the right to that, even if he messed it up.

Moving through the crowd, he spotted Amber. Chance was on one side of her and Logan on the other, his arm slung around her shoulder.

Gritting his teeth, Monty took out his phone and sent another text to her brother.

Chance dug out his cell, looked at the screen and shoved the phone back in his pocket.

He was being deliberately ignored. First by Amber and now her brother.

Giving her space, allowing her to decide when and where they spoke, hadn't worked for months. He was done using that tactic. Ever since he woke up in the hospital yesterday, a clock ticked in his soul, making him feel time was running out. He couldn't afford to wait any longer.

Monty cut through the crowd, weaving around people. "Excuse me," he said several times, drawing closer to the front near the stage, where Amber was headed. He pushed through gently, ignoring the wary glances he drew once people recognized him.

Under normal circumstances, he loved living in a small town where everyone knew each other, but once he was suspected of murder, those friendly neighbors, some of whom had known him since he was a child, had turned on him quicker than a pack of wolves on a wounded stag.

For a second he lost them, but then he homed in on the group standing a bit taller than most. Matt, Holden, Logan and Chance stood out clustered together. He made his way over to them.

Grace was next to Holden, who held Kayce. Matt was singing along with the choir to the baby and making funny hand gestures that had the little one giggling. Hannah was off at the ranch, searching it from top to bottom with Waylon and as many officers as they could muster.

Narrowing his eyes at Chance, he slipped an arm past him and caught Amber's elbow, drawing her gaze. "Hey, can we talk? I really need to speak with you."

Logan flashed him a surly expression that he wanted to knock off his face, but his brother was only being protective of Amber. How could he not respect him for that?

"Talk about what?" she asked, like she didn't have the foggiest idea.

"Everything. Yesterday morning and the way it looked." Monty glanced around, needing to be discreet, but the crowd made it a challenge. "What's happening to me," he said, in code for the fact he was accused of murder. But they also had other things to discuss. "About us. That thing after your father's funeral." Namely, the hot sex they'd had and how the thought of it, of her, had been torturing him for months until he woke up with a dead body yesterday morning, changing the priority of his concerns. "Just give me a minute."

She didn't look amenable.

Then Logan dared to add, "You don't owe him anything. In fact, it's the other way around."

Fighting hard to ignore his brother, he stayed focused on the person who mattered right now. "Please. I'm begging." Something he never did.

She held up a finger. "One minute."

Cupping her arm, he glared at his brother before he led her to the side of the stage by the stairs she would have to use in a few minutes when his mother called her up.

It wasn't ideal. Brianne and Eddie were standing close. The chief of staff mooned over his mom's assistant. She fed him a piece of a doughnut and brushed crumbs from his mustache. He thanked her with a peck on the lips.

"Would you mind giving us a minute?" he asked them.

Brianne pursed her lips at the intrusion into the space they had occupied first, but Eddie smiled and ushered her off in the direction of the food trucks.

"I'm not sure what you could possibly have to say about sleeping with Pandora," Amber said, "but I know you didn't kill her."

"But there was nothing between me and Pandora. I've never slept with her. I need you to know that."

"Really? You expect me to believe that?" Amber shook her head, pursing her rosy, bow-shaped lips. "Please don't try to spoon-feed me the same hogwash you used with your family about her not being your type. I know better. Svelte blondes and redheads, who only need you to look their way and smile to spread their legs, is precisely what you like."

He loved the fire in her, even when it burned in his direction hot enough to scorch, especially when it burned in his direction.

"Sleeping with her would've hurt you. That's why she wasn't my type," he said. Her gulp was audible. Maybe he was getting through to her. "I'd never do that to you. Never. I promise."

Those striking hazel eyes that were an intriguing mix of brown, green and amber framed by inky, thick lashes widened, boring into his. Her tongue darted out, wetting her pink lips.

And he was struck by how pretty she was. Not drop-dead gorgeous, but the kind of face that only got better with age. That caught and held his attention. Always had. A head full of dark curly hair that she kept wild and free. A soft brown complexion, dimples when she smiled, and when she did, her face glowed with an intoxicating enthusiasm that made him grin, too.

Averting her gaze, she shoved hair behind her ear with a trembling hand. Was her blood sugar low again? Or was he to blame, making her nervous?

But that look of vulnerability, the complete lack of guile in her, the dichotomy of sweet and sassy, had won him over.

"Please, Amber. I need you." Now more than ever and he wasn't going to get her, not really, not the in the way he wanted until they hashed things out.

"Need me for what?" She stared at her boots. "You've got your family. And Chance found one of the best criminal attorneys for you."

He wanted her friendship. Her support. Her affection. And so much more. "It's difficult to explain."

"Now isn't the right time to talk."

The choir finished their song.

His mother went up to the microphone at the podium. "Everyone, let's show the women's auxiliary choir how much we enjoyed their performance."

The crowd broke into a raucous round of applause.

"I agree," he said to Amber, unable to disregard the stares he garnered, ranging from leery to hateful. "We should speak somewhere quiet. In private." Without the prying eyes of the entire town. "But you've ghosted me for weeks. Months. When I called you last night, you sent it straight to voice mail. How about after you light the tree we go somewhere together?"

She looked around. "I can't. I'm exhausted and not feeling well," she said, still not meeting his eyes. "I need to go home and get some sleep."

"Then when?"

Amber shrugged. "I don't know." The fear in her voice was clear.

She was scared he would hurt her again and she had every reason to be guarded, but he had grown up while she was gone. Made changes. The old him was a bull in a china shop when it came to going after something or someone he wanted.

Maybe she was expecting that from him.

With her, he didn't want to come on too strong and have her thinking it was because of the land. He'd learned from his mistakes and would never mislead her, never let her believe something that wasn't true ever again.

"Listen, I've been a very patient man." Too patient. Too passive.

"Good for you. Would you like a trophy with your name engraved on it?"

He swallowed back a groan.

His mother was talking about Christmas, gearing up to bring Amber onto the stage.

"Your son is a murderer!" a man called out from somewhere in the crowd. "He should be in jail! Why hasn't he been arrested?"

Monty spotted the guy. Barrel-chested. Goatee. Stood out like a sore thumb. But several in the crowd echoed the man's sentiments.

"My son has not been charged with any crime," his mother said. "Every single person is innocent until *proven guilty.* Let's get back to the festivities and the reason we've all gathered here as neighbors, friends, a community that stands strong together, united in any adversity."

Needing to get out of the public eye, he turned back to Amber to pin her down on a place and time. "This is important. Come on. You can't avoid me forever, Tinker."

Her head whipped up at him, her angry eyes locking with his. "That's how you still see me, isn't it? An overly emotional fairy, stuck in never-never land, in love with Peter Pan, destined to only be his sidekick. Well, I have news for you. I have a life waiting for me back in Texas, and I deserve more, I deserve better, than the likes of you, Montgomery Beaumont Powell," she said, knocking the wind from his lungs.

"Now it's time for the moment you've all been waiting for," his mother announced over the mic. "The lighting of the holiday tree. Amber Sofia Reyes, the daughter of Carlos Reyes, a pillar of the community who recently lost his long battle with cancer, will do the honor. Come on up here, honey."

Amber spun away from him, hurried up the stairs and joined his mother at the podium.

Monty turned, scanning the crowd for the man who had shouted accusations and riled up the crowd, but he was gone.

"Three!" His mother began the countdown as Amber's hand hovered over the big red button, ready to push it. "Two. One."

Amber pressed the button.

The tree lit up in a dazzling blaze of color in tandem with fireworks going off. But over the "oohs" and "aahs" a sharp crack punctured the air. Monty's mind registered the danger as reflex took over.

A gunshot.

"Get down! Gunfire!" Monty was already up the stairs, bolting across the stage.

His father grabbed his mother, rushing her to safety. From the corner of his eye, he spotted the rest of his family, scrambling for cover as the crowd dispersed in screaming chaos.

Pop! Pop!

Monty lunged for Amber and threw her to the ground behind the podium, pinning her underneath him to protect her.

The sound of the shots echoed in his head. He remained in that position, shielding her, waiting, listening.

"Monty, I need to move," she said in a strained breath, like he was crushing her.

He hadn't realized he'd put so much of his weight on her, and rolled off. "Stay down." He peered out from behind the podium, looking to see if the gunman was still out there.

Then it occurred to him that with all the accusations and hateful glares, whoever had opened fire had probably been targeting him. Maybe by trying to protect Amber, he was the one endangering her. He scanned the area to make sure it was safe for her to get up.

Police were fanning out. His family were all okay. Grace, the baby, his brothers, Chance—no one appeared injured. *Thank goodness.*

It looked all clear.

His mother broke free from his father and dashed out from behind a position of safety, rushing toward him. He was about to tell her that he was fine, but she ran right past him and dropped to her knees beside Amber.

"Are you all right?" his mother asked.

"I think so," Amber said, but her voice sounded pained and exhausted to the point of tears.

Monty knelt to help her up, taking her hand.

Wincing, Amber groaned.

"What's wrong?" He checked her visually, making sure she hadn't been hit.

"She needs to go to the hospital," his mother said.

Amber shook her head. "No." She glanced at Monty before looking back at his mother. "I'm fine." She stood, using his assistance. Once she got upright, she doubled over with another grimace and held her stomach.

"Oh, God. Buck! Get the car!" his mother called out. "We'll go to the hospital and get you checked out. Just the two of us, honey, okay?"

"What's wrong?" Monty asked. "Were you hit?" He didn't see any blood. "Where were you shot?"

"I don't feel well." Amber grimaced. "Something's wrong."

"I'll go with you," Monty said.

Her eyes widened in alarm.

"No, no," his mother said, waving him off. "She's sick with a woman thing. We'll go without you. Buck! Where's your father with the car?"

As if she'd willed it, his father sped up in his mother's Hummer and screeched to halt near the curb. Thankfully, as mayor, she had a reserved spot close by.

Pain wrenched across Amber's face, and she squeezed his hand hard. "On second thought, you should come to the hospital."

"Are you sure?" he asked, panic gripping him.

She nodded. "Just in case everything isn't okay." She curled her arm around her stomach. "I'm not sick. I'm pregnant."

"Pregnant?" Monty stared at her in stunned surprise. But they hadn't slept together in months. Was she that far along? Four months?

His mother smacked the back of his head, nearly knocking off his hat. "Get her to the car."

A protective rush seized Monty's chest like a vise. He bent over and, sweeping an arm under Amber's legs, lifted her up from the stage. Then, holding her tight against him, he ran to the waiting vehicle.

Chapter Nine

Saturday, December 7
5:55 p.m.

Lying on a hospital bed in the Laramie emergency room, Amber groaned as another sharp pain sliced through her pelvic area.

Please, let the baby be all right. Please.

Monty was at her side, holding her hand.

"Is it still the same?" Holly asked, pacing back and forth. "Changed any? Worse or better?"

"It's the same. Something is wrong." Tears welled in Amber's eyes, blurring her vision. "I'm scared."

Amber had lost her mother, her father, and even Monty once. Losing this baby, too, would be more than she could be bear.

Monty brushed hair back from her face and kissed her forehead. "It's going to be all right."

"Now is not the time for empty platitudes, son, as well-meaning as they may be. We need a doctor. Right now." Holly yanked aside the curtain that afforded her a modicum of privacy in the ER bay. "I'm going to find one." She closed it and padded off.

"My mom is about to get scary and make a scene," Monty said.

Amber expected no less from Holly Powell. The woman

was a force to be reckoned with. "She has my blessing. How long have we been waiting?"

He glanced at his watch. "Twenty minutes." He peered down at her and flashed a sad smile. "Don't worry, she's going to get someone in here lickety-split." His tone was off somehow. He sounded distant, filtered.

She couldn't quite put it into words, but she didn't like it. "Monty, I want you to be here with me through this, but you're acting weird. It's making it worse."

He frowned. "Do you want me to leave?"

"No." Another pain lanced her and she hissed, breathing through it.

He kissed the back of her hand. "Is there anything I can do?" he asked, tightening his grip on her.

"I'm scared, terrified I might lose this baby. I need *you*. To act normal. To sound like you."

"I'm sorry." His brow furrowed, his face taking on the expression he got when he was thinking hard, trying to work out a problem, solve some puzzle.

"What are you thinking?" she asked. He hadn't uttered a word about the baby or the fact that she'd hidden it. Hadn't asked her a single question. "I need you to be honest." For once. "Please."

He hesitated, staring at her, looking completely lost.

"If you're angry I didn't tell you or disappointed that I'm pregnant, I'd understand." She stared down at her belly bump.

Once she discovered she was pregnant and got over the initial surprise, there had never been any doubt in her mind that she would keep this child. Raise it. Cherish it. She'd loved Monty since she was twelve, dreamed of marrying him, but after he'd conspired with her father to trick her into marriage so the Powells could have the land they always coveted, she hated him in equal measure. But if she were to ever have a child, it might as well be Monty's. That didn't mean he wanted this baby.

"I'm not angry. I'm not disappointed." He hesitated again.

"Then what is it? What aren't you saying? What are you thinking?" She squeezed his hand so hard he probably thought she wanted to break it. "You need to tell me the truth. Or I'll imagine the worst."

"I'm freaking out. Okay? I know that's not what you want to hear. It sure isn't what you need. Give me gunfire and deranged criminals and I'm fine. Give me fifteen thousand cattle to brand and herd and I'm great. But I woke up drugged with Pandora dead on the floor yesterday. I came this close to getting arrested. We were shot at tonight. Now I find out that I'm going to be a father. Possibly. Because I don't know what's happening with you, if the baby, my baby, *our baby*, is all right. I'm worried I hurt the two of you when I was trying to get you down behind some cover. Maybe I hit your stomach by accident." He scrubbed a hand over his face. "So I've been trying to be quiet, to be supportive, to give you what you need, not that I know what that is, and not make this about me when it has to be all about you and…" He pressed a tentative hand to her belly. "Why didn't you tell me?"

"You know why." She looked away from him and at the pale yellow curtain.

Fluorescent bulbs flickered overhead. The smell of antiseptic made her nausea flare.

"My daughter-in-law needs to be seen right this second!" Holly yelled at someone in the hall. "I know every single person sitting on the board of directors at this hospital. If a doctor isn't in bay four in the next two minutes, examining her and making sure that my unborn grandchild is okay, after we were just shot at, I'm going to start making some unpleasant phone calls."

Monty sighed. "You should've told me about the baby," he

said, his tone gentle, his voice soft. "From the way my mom acted on the stage, she already knew. Didn't you think I had a right to know, too?"

"I was going to tell you. And your mom only found out at the house yesterday."

"I get that you needed time and space." He kept using that tone of gentle compassion that made her want to dissolve into a puddle of emotion. "But I've been calling, texting, leaving notes on your front door, and you've been ghosting me for four months, using Chance as an intermediary. When were you going to tell me?"

She couldn't trust the sweet things he said. Couldn't trust his affection. Most importantly, she couldn't trust herself around him. "When the time was right."

The curtain was drawn aside. Holly stood there, letting someone pass her.

A man wearing green scrubs and a white lab coat entered the bay. He had light brown hair that was receding. Busy chewing, he held a sandwich in one hand and raised a finger from the other, indicating he needed a moment. "Sorry for the delay," he said around the food in his mouth. "The ER doctor heard the mayor's frustration and was afraid to examine you. Dr. Plinsky thought it best for an expert to come down. I'm Dr. Kevin. Like to keep it informal. I'm the head of OB-GYN."

Amber glanced at the partially eaten sandwich in his hand. "Do you need to finish eating?"

With a shake of his head, Dr. Kevin stuffed the rest of the food in his mouth and went to the sink to wash his hands. "I just finished delivering two babies back-to-back. This was my first chance to grab a bite to eat." He dried his hands, pulled on latex gloves and turned to her. "What seems to be the problem, Mrs. Powell?"

Her cheeks were suddenly on fire. "We're not married. I'm Amber Reyes."

"Oh, I see. I must've misunderstood. Everyone else can step outside and go to the waiting room if you'd like."

"I'm staying," Monty said.

Holly nodded. "Me, too."

The doctor frowned. "That's up to Ms. Reyes to decide, sir, and Mayor. We're sticklers about privacy here at the hospital. Amber, it's important that you feel free to speak openly during the examination. Clearing the bay of everyone else might be in the best interest of your health and that of your baby."

Now that Monty knew about the baby and was here beside her, she didn't want him to leave. "No, no." She shook her head. "It's okay." She tightened her grip on Monty. "If they stay, it'll save me the hassle of updating them on everything."

They might as well hear it firsthand.

"I'm afraid only one of you can stay," the doctor said.

Amber looked at Monty.

The corner of his mouth hitched in a small grin. "I'm not going anywhere."

"Mayor." Dr. Kevin turned to Holly. "You can step out to the waiting room." He drew the curtain closed. "Tell me what's going on, Amber."

"I've been having sharp pains, some dull ones, too, right around my pelvic area and belly button. At times it feels like stabbing and other moments like a tight pull."

Dr. Kevin put a blood pressure cuff on her and started the machine. "How long has this been going on?"

"There was a shooting at the tree lighting ceremony," Monty said. "I knocked her to the ground, trying to protect her, and then she was in pain." The guilt in his voice tugged at her heart.

"It actually started yesterday. I got lightheaded at the house. The room spun. And I felt a new twinge, a sort of pulling, in the lower part of my belly here." She showed him the location of the pain. "As the day wore on, it's gotten worse and

I've still been a bit dizzy. I thought it was low blood sugar. I nibbled on something, but the twinge turned into a slight stabbing. Then when I fell—"

"When I knocked you down." His voice rumbled with something that sounded like fear.

"When Monty saved me from getting shot, I protected my belly and fell on my back. But the stabbing pain has gotten bad. So has the pulling sensation. Feels like I'm having contractions."

It was far too soon for that. The baby didn't have a chance of survival outside the womb until she was at least six months.

Amber rubbed her belly. *You have to be all right, peanut.*

She wanted this child more than anything. Not for a second had it been unwelcome. She would never think of this baby as a mistake even if loving its father might have been. The conception had been completely unplanned, but a blessing in disguise. Endometriosis and surgery for it had caused scarring that blocked one of her fallopian tubes. Doctors had told her it might be extremely difficult if not next to impossible to conceive when she was ready.

In a way, the child growing inside her was really a miracle.

"Your blood pressure is elevated." Dr. Kevin removed the cuff from her arm. "Along with your heart rate. But you've just been through something stressful. How far along are you?"

"Seventeen weeks, four days."

"Any vaginal bleeding?" the doctor asked.

"No," she said, thankful for that. "I checked again when we got to the ER."

"Mind if I take a look?" He indicated her belly.

"Please do."

Dr. Kevin lifted her oversize sweater and started prodding her stomach, working clockwise.

"You've gotten so big," Monty said. "That's why you wouldn't see me."

"I honestly didn't think you'd notice," she said. "Figured you'd assume I was simply getting fatter."

"You're not fat. You're voluptuous." He flashed her a warm smile. "I like your curves."

She twisted her mouth, swallowing the word *liar*.

"It's true." Monty leaned over and brought his lips close to her ear. "Believe it or not, a man likes a woman with some meat on her bones," he whispered. "I didn't become attracted to you until you filled out in all the right places. I remember the day I first noticed. We went to the town's spring dance. You wore that skimpy sundress that revealed far too much leg and cleavage. With straps so thin I was tempted to pluck them with a finger to see if they'd snap. And that dress had bright red, plump cherries all over it. Fitted like a second skin. You didn't even wear a bra underneath. Teetered on indecent." He purred in her ear, sending tingles dancing over her skin. "Paired it with cowboy boots and a straw hat. You looked ripe enough to eat, even though you were jailbait," he drawled, his voice dipping low, making her toes curl. "I remember like it was yesterday."

This time her cheeks heated for a different reason. She'd worn it just for him. Her mother had called the dress *scandalous* and *inappropriate*, worried it would set tongues wagging in the small town, and forbade her going to the dance with it on. But her father had intervened, having the final word. He'd even sent Chance on ahead dreadfully early and called Buck, asking him if Monty could give her a ride.

She had been on cloud nine, squealing her thanks to her dad, hugging him tight, so excited to ride alone with Monty Powell in his truck. Until he showed up. Along with all his brothers—the lost boys. The guys whooped and whistled. Except for Monty. He was stone-faced, not cracking a smile, eyes hidden behind dark sunglasses, not uttering a word about the dress, barely giving her a second glance.

"Nice boots, Tinker," was all Monty had said.

And only Logan wanted to dance with her.

A stab of pain had her gripping her lower belly.

Concern etched Monty's face. He pressed a palm to her cheek, and she couldn't help but turn into his touch. What she wouldn't have given for a hug.

"Tell me, Amber, have you had much to eat or drink today?" Dr. Kevin pulled her sweater down, covering her belly.

"Crackers. A little applesauce. Lots of ginger ale. Soup for lunch."

Dr. Kevin nodded as though he was thinking. His face was inscrutable. "I have good news and bad news."

Fear jolted through her. She exchanged a worried glance with Monty.

She braced for the worst and Monty moved his palm from her cheek to grip her shoulder as if to steady her.

Dr. Kevin peeled off his gloves and tossed them in the trash. "The good news is I think it's only dehydration and the usual discomfort that comes as your uterus grows and stretches the supporting ligaments."

A breath of relief punched from her lips. Her little peanut was going to be okay. Monty smiled down at her and kissed the top of her head.

"Thank goodness," Holly said from the other side of the curtain.

Dr. Kevin raised an eyebrow. "I can't believe she's still here," he whispered.

"That's because you don't know my mother."

"Dehydration can be problematic any time, but it's especially concerning during pregnancy," the doctor said. "Not only do you need more water than usual, but your baby needs water, too. Not staying properly hydrated can lead to serious complications. Neural tube defects. Low amniotic fluid. Premature labor. Poor production of breast milk. But even something as mild as dizziness can be an issue if you were to faint."

The number of things that could go wrong was staggering. She should have known better. Three different baby books were on her nightstand, and she had read through two of them. She'd found an OB-GYN in Cheyenne to keep it quiet, and was taking prenatal vitamins, going on long walks for exercise, and had cut out fatty foods and desserts. Well, most desserts. When she could tolerate them, she was guilty of indulging.

"What's the bad news?" Holly asked from the hall.

Dr. Kevin shook his head and mouthed, *unbelievable*. "The bad news is you need to carry a water bottle around and constantly sip on it. That means you're going to run to the bathroom a lot. Especially as the baby gets bigger and presses down on your bladder."

A small price to pay for a healthy child. "Okay. I'll buy one tomorrow." She would do whatever was necessary.

"No need, honey," Holly said. "I'm texting Buck now to go get one before the store closes. Thirty-two ounces with time markers to help you remember."

Dr. Kevin blew out a breath. "The time markers are a good idea to help you remember," he said with a thread of annoyance. "I also want you to try to eat more. Get in some protein, plenty of veggies and fruit. If you don't, a baby will suck its mother dry of nutrients in order to survive."

He made an unborn child sound like a vampire.

"Does she need to be on bed rest?" Monty asked.

"No. I don't see any reason for that. But stress should be kept to an absolute minimum. I would like to take a look at the baby because of your fall. To be certain everything is okay and that there's no placenta abruption. I'll get you started on an IV to replenish your system. Then we can do an ultrasound, if you'd like."

"Yes," she and Monty said in unison.

The doctor got to work setting up the IV drip.

She met Monty's gaze and swore more than affection was reflected in his eyes.

He would finally get to see the baby growing inside her. A joy she had denied him by not telling him.

All she wanted was to protect herself and this child, but maybe she had done more harm than good by giving him the cold shoulder. No matter what happened between them, they were going to be parents, and she wanted him to start bonding with and loving this baby as soon as possible.

But she couldn't help but wonder whether a part of him might resent her for getting pregnant.

"This should help you start to feel better quickly, in a manner of minutes. I'll go get the ultrasound machine." Dr. Kevin left.

In the hall, Holly said to the doctor, "I have some questions for you." Her voice faded as she followed him away.

"I need to ask you something," she said, not quite sure how to put the words together. Typical questions like if he wanted to be a father, to have a baby with her, wouldn't work.

The man was a paradox. Half of him driven by duty and honor. In that regard, he'd give the right answers to conventional questions. Declare he was going to marry her. Do right by the child. But the other half of him was compelled to act in the opposite manner of what was expected of him.

If he felt forced, he'd only be miserable.

She wanted this child to be a source of happiness for both its parents. Not one of obligation. And certainly not a convenient way for the Powells to get their hands on the Reyes land.

"Ask me anything," he said, his voice soft, his expression open, his eyes warm.

"Why did you sleep me with after the funeral? Don't worry, you can be honest. You won't hurt my feelings." Not any more than he already had.

He looked taken aback. "Nature, I guess."

Her throat went tight, and she cursed how wrong she was about the depths to which he was capable of wounding her. The nonchalance of his three-word response broke her heart.

This was torture. Loving someone, desperate to have him love her back and want the life she desired when he didn't.

"Nature?" she asked. Like she had been a mare in heat and him a stallion, following instinct.

Monty shrugged. "Yeah. What are you getting at? If this is about the land, it had nothing to do with that."

"Because it was nature." Sounded so much better. Frustration welled. She shook her head and clenched her hands. "Just say it. You were only comforting me that night." She struggled to hold back tears. "It was pity sex. Yes, you do want the land, for your family, but you didn't sign up for a kid." The terms of the trust were that the marriage had to last two years, no children required. Then he could bail. "You didn't want to be tied to me for the rest of your life. I know you regret sleeping with me."

"What?" A low chuckle rolled from him. "That's not true."

"Stop lying to me. I heard you at the house. You specifically used the words *mistake* and *regret* in the context of having sex with me." *In front of everyone!*

The wound in her heart opened anew at the same time another pang jabbed her pelvis, but the intensity was less than earlier.

Monty sat on the edge of the bed, pressed a palm to her cheek and cupped her jaw, drawing her gaze to his. "I never got to finish what was on my mind because someone interrupted me. I did make a mistake with you. A big one. I regret ever laying a finger on you without telling you the truth first. It was one thing to take you out and spend time with you, but quite another to get intimate. I should've been honest before we made love much less before I proposed. I'm sorry I hurt

you. I ruined everything. Blew up the life we could've had."
He heaved a breath. "You've got a right to believe what you
want. Except for one thing. I didn't sleep with you after your
father's funeral out of pity."

She squeezed her eyes shut to keep tears from falling.
"Then you did it because of his will." She hated that land and
the river on it.

"I am not a manipulator."

"Oh, no?" Tightness pulled at her belly. Wincing, she rubbed
the bump. "Could've fooled me. Ten years ago, you made me
believe that you loved me. That you wanted to marry me."

"Made you believe?" he asked. "Or let you?"

She glared at him. "Are you trying to spin this back onto
me somehow?"

"It takes two, sweetie. You have some culpability in what
happened. Not much. Maybe the size of a mustard seed while
I'm responsible for the bushel, but it's there."

Amber rolled her eyes. "You misled me. How is that my
fault?"

"Did I ever tell you I loved you?"

She thought about it and squirmed. "Well, no."

"Did you ever ask yourself, or me, why would a man who's
never said those words propose to you?"

She'd gotten so caught up in the butterflies and the romance
and the fairy tale she'd dreamed of finally coming true that she
didn't want to ask. "But you made me feel like you loved me."

"I've always had deep feelings for you." He brushed her
jaw with his knuckles. "I only hid it well."

"Why? If that's true, why would you hide how you felt?"

He took off his hat and sat it on a table, which meant this
was going to get serious. Real.

"Two reasons," he said. "First, Logan was in love with you.
I was the eldest. The one who gave up toys, clothes, the extra
dessert, who took tasks that the younger ones didn't want to

do. If there was something we both wanted, I let whichever brother who desired it have it. No way, no how, was I going to flirt with you or date you and rub his nose in it. No, sirree. That might not make sense to you because you're the youngest and a girl, the apple of Carlos Reyes's eye, and always got everything you wanted."

Except for you.

"It makes sense, in a weird way," she said grudgingly. "What's the second reason?"

"That one's personal."

The only thing stopping her from screaming her frustration was this baby. Her lungs burned as she inhaled. "Hiding things from me is how you ruined everything before. I need the truth."

"This is true." He leaned in, gently gripping her chin between his thumb and forefinger. "Back then, when we were going out, the more time we spent alone, talking, having fun, *having sex*, taking long drives with no destination and enjoying the journey together, the more I felt for you until I loved you, so deeply. More than anything. But then I lost you."

She dropped her head back on the pillow, wanting to believe him. But how could she? Only someone glutton for punishment would. "Fool me once shame on you. Fool me twice shame on me."

Monty sighed. "After your father's funeral, I found you in the barn, brushing his horse." He put a palm on her wrist and leaned in close, sending a rush of warmth spreading through her chest. "I hugged you and you started crying. I was wiping away your tears, feeling sorry for your loss."

So it was *pity.* The man was an incorrigible liar.

"But…" His voice trailed off. "This is going to sound selfish—I felt more sorry for myself because I'd let you go and didn't run after you. I've regretted it every day, every single second, of these past ten years. When we were in the barn, alone, I held you and looked down into your face and I wanted you. The way a man wants a woman. *Nature*. Wanted to kiss you, to hold you, to be inside you again," he said, and her stomach swooped.

She swallowed, blinking through a shimmer of tears. Why was he doing this? Saying everything she wanted to hear? Reeling her in when she was vulnerable? She didn't know if she could go down this path again. It had taken years of therapy to recover from the betrayal. She wanted to trust the father of her child, the man she desperately loved, but she didn't want to get hurt again.

Meeting his gaze, she was thunderstruck by what she saw in his eyes. Regret. Anguish. Desire.

"Amber." He cupped her face with his hands. "That night I needed to show you what you meant to me and how much I still love you."

And then he kissed her.

She squeezed her thighs together to ease the ache of longing that spread in an instant.

His lips were hot and firm and certain. A mix of fire and hunger. He kissed her like he was starving. Drinking her in with each stroke of his tongue that plunged deeper, sliding against hers in the sweetest heat, melting her to pieces.

Chapter Ten

This was his woman. His future wife. The mother of his unborn child. And Monty let her know it the only way he could. With this kiss, he told her all the things he couldn't say because she wouldn't believe him. All the things he wanted—to devour her, to take her to his bed, to have her body beneath his. To lose himself in her. To hear her cry out his name.

To hold her. To love her.

To have a second chance.

A chance to get it right.

The sound of the curtain being drawn had them jerking apart.

The doctor cleared his throat as he wheeled the ultrasound machine into the bay. Based on the wide grin on his mother's face, she had also seen them.

He looked down at Amber and swallowed, his mouth going dry again. In her eyes, he saw lust and desire and possibly the spark of forgiveness. Everything he'd hoped to see.

Hell, that kiss should have taken away some of her doubts. The chemistry they had—he'd never experienced anything like it. And right then, he'd never wanted anything so much in his life as he wanted to kiss her again.

"How are you feeling?" Dr. Kevin closed the curtain in Holly's face. "Any better?"

"Much better actually. The twinges and pangs are less frequent. The intensity decreased, too."

"Good. That's exactly what I was hoping to hear. Are we ready to do an ultrasound?"

She nodded.

"Yes," Monty said. He needed to make sure Amber and the baby were okay.

The doctor turned on the machine and washed his hands again.

"I'm sorry you missed the first one," she said, looking up at him. "You had a right to be there. It's your baby, too."

"It's okay." He understood why she'd kept the truth from him. "When did you do it?"

"The doctor recommended at seven weeks. The baby is due May sixteenth."

A May baby. "Did you go alone?"

"Chance came with me."

Of course, her brother had the whole time. It explained why he had agreed to act as a go-between, not letting him in the house, but passing on his messages. Normally, Chance didn't like to get involved in other people's affairs. Not that Monty could be angry with him for supporting his sister. She had needed someone to be there for her when she probably worried she'd have to contend with the full force of the Powell clan.

"Well, I'm here now." He took her hand in his. From here on out, they were going to do this together. He couldn't wait to see his baby for the first time.

Dr. Kevin put on gloves. "Pull your sweater up for me and lower your waistband. Sorry, the gel is going to be cold."

As Amber adjusted her clothes, Monty noticed her hands trembling slightly. "Are you hungry?"

"Yeah. I find it easier to eat a little bit at a time."

"Craving anything?" he asked, knowing his mother was still eavesdropping.

"This IV must be doing the trick because I'm craving a hamburger smothered in ketchup. And ice cream. A chocolate milkshake. But I know I shouldn't have it."

Dr. Kevin picked up the gel. "Sounds like you haven't been eating much lately. A burger is perfect. Full of protein, iron, zinc and several B vitamins. And there is nothing wrong with a milkshake as long as you're not drinking one every day. You and the baby both need the calcium."

Monty leaned in close to her ear. "How much do you want to bet that a burger and chocolate shake will be waiting for you once you're done here?" He gestured to the curtain with his head.

She smiled bright and warm, full of pure joy, and his heart danced in his chest as he grinned back at her.

The doctor moved the sweater higher and her waistband even lower.

Monty hadn't been lying about loving her figure. Full curves in all the right places that he couldn't get enough of. He wondered what she would look like with her belly big and round, heavy with his child and her breasts too full for his hands. Even sexier was his guess.

He stroked her hair, running his fingers through the lustrous, soft strands.

Dr. Kevin squirted goo on her abdomen. Amber gasped.

"Sorry, I know it's cold," he said.

"It's all right. You did warn me. I just hadn't been prepared for how cold. The gel my OB uses is warm."

"Who's your doctor?"

"Jennie Jankowski."

"Out in Cheyenne?" Dr. Kevin asked, and Amber nodded. "She's great, but if you're planning to have this baby around here, you should find someone local. Otherwise, although you may develop a good, trusting relationship with Jennie, she probably won't be the one to deliver the baby. Having a stranger help you bring your child into the world can be disconcerting."

"I guess I'm not sure where I'll be when this peanut is born."

She wasn't thinking of going back to Texas, was she?

Not pregnant with his kid and alone.

The doctor pressed the probe to her belly and moved it around while staring at the screen until a weird throbbing noise echoed in the room as a grainy image flickered on the screen.

"Looks good so far," Dr. Kevin said. "Nice, strong heartbeat, this one. No worries there."

"Is it supposed to be that fast?" Monty wondered.

"One hundred forty-five beats per minute is perfectly normal." The doctor grinned. "Should be almost twice the mother's heart rate."

"Is everything else okay?" Amber asked.

Dr. Kevin moved the probe around her belly, staring at the screen. "There's the head, the arms, legs," he said.

It looked like a baby. Not just some peanut-shaped blob the way he'd expected.

A perfectly shaped, tiny hand came into view. Monty leaned in toward the screen, his chest coming close to Amber's head. If his mother peered in now to catch a glimpse of the scene, she might naturally assume there was no question this would work out, the two of them as a happy couple, and for a wild, hopeful moment he wished with all his heart it would be that easy.

Even though her father had thought his last legal wishes would bring them together, and it had ten years ago, it kept them apart now.

"Everything looks normal. Very healthy. I'm not seeing any issues with the placenta," Dr. Kevin said, and Monty heard his mother exhale in relief. "Your baby is a little over five and a half inches long and almost seven ounces. Hey, fun fact, your baby's fingerprints are now formed."

Amber grinned from ear to ear, and Monty lit up. They were going to have a baby. The specifics still had to be worked out, but they were a family. Despite everything else going on, this was something to be celebrated.

"Would you like to know the baby's gender?"

Tipping her head back, she smiled at him and shrugged. "I don't know. This could be a once-in-a-lifetime surprise. Maybe we should wait. What do you think?"

He was chomping at the bit to know, but it was Amber's decision. "Whatever you want to do, that's what I want. A once-in-a-lifetime surprise sounds nice."

"You're disappointed," she said. "I can hear it in your voice. You want to know."

"This isn't about me. I'm happy to wait."

"Be honest. Please." She studied his face. "What do you want?"

This was a test. In his gut, he knew it. He had to be honest in all things. "Whether it's a boy or girl doesn't matter. Either way, I'll be thrilled, but I do want to know. I just don't want to spoil a surprise for you. Ruin it for you."

"This baby is healthy. As long as he or she stays that way, nothing is ruined." She looked at the doctor. "Tell us."

Dr. Kevin moved the probe again, making some adjustments. "Sure you want to know? You can always wait for a later appointment."

"I'm sure. We're together now. I don't know about the next ultrasound," she said, and something in his chest pinched.

She still doubted him. Much more than he thought.

The doctor pointed to the screen. "There you go. Can you see the package?"

"Do you mean…" Excitement competed with anticipation, leaving him speechless. He waited for confirmation.

Dr. Kevin nodded.

Monty's eyes watered. "A boy." His voice was choked. "Amber, we're going to have a son."

Her bottom lip trembled and tears welled in her eyes. "A son," she echoed, in amazement or disbelief, or perhaps a bit of both. Pressing her hands to her chest, she stared at the monitor before turning back to him. She sent him a tremulous smile.

Monty didn't hesitate to bend over and give her a gentle kiss on her lips.

"Buck, it's a boy!" his mother squealed. She must've called his father on the phone.

Monty pulled away, beaming at Amber, and they both laughed.

The doctor raised his eyebrows. "I forgot she was there," he whispered.

Staring deep into her eyes, Monty wished he could name all the emotions flooding his heart. He looked back at the screen, awestruck. The baby was so tiny. So fragile.

And someone had fired a gun several times, endangering Amber and his little one.

He needed to figure out what was going on and fast. It was the only way to keep them safe.

"Would you like me to print a picture?" Dr. Kevin asked.

"Yes," they said in unison.

"One for each of us," Amber clarified. "We're not together."

Dr. Kevin's smile deflated right along with Monty's hope. He had more work to do than he realized. Regret siphoned some of his elation, but he hid it well, not wanting to dampen Amber's spirits.

"Please print an extra one for me," his mother called out.

The doctor handed one to each of them along with some paper towels for Amber. "The IV should be finished in another fifteen to twenty minutes. I'll have Dr. Plinsky get your discharge paperwork ready for you."

"Thank you." Amber wiped the gel from her belly. "We appreciate you rushing through your late dinner."

"I'm happy to assuage your worries. Be sure to eat, drink lots of water and get plenty of rest."

"I will."

Smiling, the doctor handed his mother an ultrasound picture on the way out.

Monty took the paper towels from Amber and tossed them in the trash. "Go to the waiting room, Mom." His tone brooked no argument. "I'm serious."

"I'm going," she said, with a smile and a nod. "We got you a burger and milkshake, honey. Do you want me to bring it to you?"

"Thank you," Amber said. "But I'll wait to eat on the way home."

"Okay. If you change your mind, text me." His mom waved and shut the curtain.

Monty sat back down on the bed next to her. "I want us to be together," he said, plainly.

Cringing, she squeezed her eyes shut. "Don't. Please don't." She huffed a breath. "Monty, don't do this—talk about marriage. I should've known better. You can't just be happy that the baby is healthy. That's it's going to be a boy. Can you? You're never satisfied with halfway. You always want it all. This is why I've dreaded telling you, because I knew you'd go caveman on me when I can't trust a single word that comes out of your lying mouth."

"I love you, Amber Reyes."

Her wary gaze flashed up to him and she looked as though she was holding her breath.

His timing was wrong. No, it sucked. But he'd put it out there and now he had to double down. "Did you hear me? I've never said that before to anyone."

"I heard you." Her voice was soft, her tone skeptical. "Want a trophy for that, too, *Peter Pan*?"

Frustration bubbled in Monty's gut. Enough was enough. "Listen, woman, this stops right here. You're not Tinker Bell. I'm not Peter Pan and I'm not some crude Neanderthal from the Stone Age either." He was a cowboy who'd finally gotten his head screwed on straight. "This isn't a fairy tale. It's messy. It's ugly. People make mistakes. Goodness knows I've made a lot of them. But this is also beautiful. And it's real. This is us, for better or for worse. We're going to have a baby. That makes us family. For life. Whether we get married or not. But I *want* to marry you. And not out of duty or honor or to get the land."

"Then why? Why do you love me? Why do you want to marry me?"

He had an answer at the ready because he'd spent many a night, tossing and turning, pondering the same thing. "I think of my life in terms of B.A.R. and A.A.R. Before Amber Reyes and after Amber Reyes. Before we got together, I was fine. Thought I was, anyway, content with my life just as it was. After you left, there was a gaping hole. Like a sucking chest wound. I became painfully aware that I was lonely. Miserable, if I'm being honest."

Raw emotion gleamed in her eyes, but she still looked dubious.

Silence stretched between them.

Taking a breath, he resolved to try harder. "It was kind of like watching the *Wizard of Oz*. Everything is black-and-white and looks pretty good until it changes to Technicolor. That's what you are for me. Every color of the spectrum in high definition, brightening and enriching my life. I'd be lying if I said I tried to move on. I didn't even bother. In my gut, I knew it'd be futile. I've just been existing. Passing time. Waiting for you. Now you're back." He put a hand to her belly. "Pregnant with my son. I need you, sweetheart. I'm miserable, sick down in my soul, without you."

Tears streamed from her eyes and her bottom lip trembled once more. "Before my father made the land become an issue and you asked me out, you claim you had feelings for me."

He nodded. "I did. Took a while for me to realize it was more than lust. It was in the way I tried to look after you. Protect you. Help you with anything that you needed. Just wanting to be near you. It was coming from a place of me loving you for years." All along. Way before their parents meddled.

"Then what's the second reason, besides Logan, why you never acted on those feelings? No more secrets. No hiding anything from me."

For her to believe, he was going to have to open up and lay himself bare. He got to his feet and peeked through the curtain into the hall, checking to make sure his mother was gone.

Satisfied she wasn't lurking within earshot, he sat back down beside Amber.

He wasn't proud of his reason, which wasn't anything noble, and that was why he classified it as personal.

Lowering his head, he pinched the bridge of his nose. "Since I was little, I was told who I was and what I was going to be. Buck and Holly Powell's eldest. Born to be a rancher. Destined to carry on the legacy. I'm sure you've noticed I don't like to be told what to do."

"I have. Kind of hard not to."

He took her hand. "I had an eye for you something fierce since you wore that cherry sundress, but Logan's interest forced me to keep my cool and my distance, like I said. But one day I overheard our parents talking about how you fancied me and how good we'd be together. How wonderful it would be if we got married and had kids. The Reyes and Powell land becoming one since neither you nor Chance wanted to be ranchers. They had my whole life mapped out for me.

Choosing my vocation, choosing my wife. Then I found myself pushing against that, too. *Real hard*." From an early age, since he could ride a horse, he'd decided for himself who he was going to be. What he was going to do. "I set my mind against being with you. Told myself all sorts of lies, like you were too young, sex with you would be boring." His eyes flew up and he stared at her, horrified to see hurt in her gaze. "Idiotic nonsense I tried to believe to stay away from you. Making love with you is perfect. Sometimes sweet and slow. Sometimes dirty, hot and wild." She brought him such pleasure, opening herself, holding nothing back, and he endeavored to do likewise. "I dream about it. A lot. Anyway, I couldn't see past those two reasons—Logan's feelings and being told I should be with you—until we were actually forced together. Sounds foolish, I know."

"It doesn't." She whisked the tears from her eyes. "Simply sounds like you."

Drawing in a breath of relief, he was glad she knew him so well. "You believe me?"

"I want to. Really, I do. More than you know. But…" She shook her head. "How can I?"

The land. The river. *The trust.*

Pain lodged in his chest. He would do anything to reassure her. "I can prove it to you. In less than thirty days, if we're not married, the land will go to Pandora's next of kin. Her mother. We let it happen. Then when you believe in my feelings, when you're ready to say yes, I'll propose again. Whether that's in two months, two years, or twenty."

Her mouth fell open, and she reeled back. "You can't be serious. You wouldn't give up everything for me. You love that land. And it means so much to your family. It would devastate your parents."

The land he'd grown up on was like gravity for him. Grounding him. Keeping him steady. Calling him always. Being out there on horseback, wrangling cattle, gave him a sense of satisfaction, of purpose, like nothing else ever had. "I love my parents. I love that ranch. But I love you more. You and this baby are everything to me. All that matters."

Staring at him, she looked stunned. "They'd never allow it. Buck and Holly would coerce and push and plead until we got married just to keep that land from going to Fiona and you know it."

A valid point. Buck and Holly were resourceful. Persuasive, too.

An idea came to him. His parents would hate him for it, but it might be the only solution. "Once we figure out what's going on and clear my name of any suspicion of murder, we leave town together. Go to Texas. Without telling anyone anything. I mean no one. Not even Chance." If word got out, they'd be in a pressure cooker. "Simply pack our bags and leave one night. And if you think that they'd follow us and harass us, then we go somewhere else until the deadline passes and it's too late."

"Monty." Amber stiffened. "I can't ask you to make that kind of sacrifice."

"You didn't ask. I need to do this to prove to you this is real and how much I love you."

"They'll never understand. They'll never forgive us. Forgive me."

He gave her a sad smile. "Yes, they will."

She shook her head slowly, unconvinced.

"Once the dust settles, after they've sold the cattle, and thousands of acres of our land since they won't need it, they will forgive us. Because of the baby you're carrying." He rubbed her belly. "They'll want to see him. They can only do that if they're nice to both of us." Might be asking a bit much. "At least civil. I won't have them giving you the stink eye or saying a cross word about you." They could curse his name if it made them feel any better.

She tore her gaze from him. Wringing her hands, she considered it.

"Give me this chance and I won't let you down." He cupped her face. "Not ever again. Take this leap with me. What do you say?"

Her swallow was audible, her cheeks going rosy, her eyes luminous. "Yes."

"Yes?"

She nodded. "I love you. I want us to be family."

Growling with soul-deep satisfaction and relief, he pulled her close and crushed his mouth to hers. He closed his eyes and reveled in the kiss, in the sultry jasmine scent of her, in the feel of her rounded baby bump pressed against his abdomen. Luxuriated in the moment. This was bliss—the quiet connection to the one woman who'd always been meant for him.

His heart drummed a frenzied rhythm against his ribs. Every muscle in his body went taut, vibrating with anticipation, straining with need so strong he ached down to his bones.

But thoughts of Pandora and the shots fired sprang to mind. He clung tighter to Amber, unable to fight the sense of helplessness rolling through him. In the pit of his stomach, he felt this might be the calm before the storm.

Chapter Eleven

Saturday, December 7
8:08 p.m.

The Shooting Star Ranch had been turned upside down and inside out and Waylon had nothing to show for it. He climbed behind the steering wheel of his truck. Hannah jumped into the passenger seat. They'd driven over together since they had to go back to the station to fill out paperwork.

He pulled out, leading the caravan of LPD cops off the ranch.

"That was a complete waste of time," Hannah said.

The hint of smugness in her tone irked him. "Maybe the flip phone the state police found in his locker and delivered to us will have something on it."

"And maybe it's just a spare phone." Hannah shook her head. "The guys didn't have to leave such a mess back there. Looks like a tornado ripped through every residence."

"I'm sure they have people to clean things up. Right? Staff? Servants?"

"No, they don't. Not in the way you mean."

He scoffed. "You expect me to believe that Holly Powell is scrubbing toilets?" he asked with a chuckle.

"There was a time when she did, but Buck and Holly have help now that they're older. Monty is going to have to clean his own cottage."

"Boo-hoo. Cry me a river."

She shifted toward him. "What about Holden and Grace? They'll have to clean their place, too, since you insisted on executing the full scope of the warrant. She's eight, almost nine months pregnant and they have a fourteen-month-old baby."

"Put your violin away, Delaney. The lawful search was a part of the job, and the mess came with the territory. You were standing right next to me when I issued the orders. I didn't tell anyone to get nasty about it." Though he did feel bad for Grace, who was pregnant and had a toddler to contend with, and Holden, whom he liked.

Holden lacked pretense and didn't have the same egotistical swagger as Monty.

"True, but you did seem to pick every available officer with a grudge against the Powells," she said. "You knew what was going to happen."

"I think they'll survive." He switched the radio on low. "You didn't happen to give them a heads-up about the search, did you?" He quirked an eyebrow at her.

"Monty was found with a dead body. A reasonable, rational expectation would be for a search warrant to be executed. Do you really think they needed me to do the math, two plus two equals four? Simple enough without my help."

Popping a piece of gum in his mouth, he restrained a chuckle at her continued avoidance of answering his questions regarding that family. "Do you want to know what I think?"

"Of course, I do, partner."

Sarcasm duly noted. "I think you told them that the search was going to happen before they gave you the heave-ho from the family meeting yesterday." He would've moved the timeline up if he'd had the necessary personnel available.

Delaney had extended the courtesy of giving him a heads-up about the meeting, which he appreciated, but he wasn't a fool.

"If I was so helpful to them, why do you suppose they kicked me out?"

"Because you're conflicted. They can smell it on you, the same way I can."

She straightened in her seat and opened another energy drink. "I know where I stand."

"Want to enlighten me as to which side that's on?"

"The side of truth." Her phone chimed. She took it out. "Monty's financials are in."

He gave her time to scroll through it. The silence was welcome. Trading barbs with her was exhausting.

"Anything of interest?" Regardless of her answer, he'd comb through it himself later.

"Possibly." She looked over at him. "What time did the outdoor security camera at Pandora's show her and Monty arriving?"

"Ten thirty."

"He used his debit card to pay at the Howling Wolf Roadhouse just before that."

"Time?"

"Four minutes past ten."

"We've got ourselves a lead. Get on the radio and let the others know we're going to peel off." The turn for the street that led to the roadhouse was about to come up soon.

Hannah passed along the message.

Once they made their turn, the others continued to the police station. The parking lot at the Howling Wolf was half-full. Security cameras mounted on the outside covered the lot and probably the road in front as well.

They climbed out and headed inside. Typical dive bar. Dim lighting. Shabby decor. Darts. Pool. Food and drink. He preferred to grab beer outside of town in Wayward Bluffs where he lived.

He wouldn't call the place seedy but wouldn't be surprised if drugs were sold out of it either.

They approached the bartender. A lanky guy covered in tattoos drying a glass.

"I'm Detective Wright. This is Detective Delaney. Were you working Thursday night?" he asked, and the guy nodded. "What's your name?"

"Finn."

"Was this guy in here that evening?" Hannah whipped out a photo of Monty on her phone.

"Yeah. Monty is in here every Thursday like clockwork."

"Oh, yeah." Waylon leaned against the bar. "Describe a regular Thursday night for him. What time does he arrive and leave? What does he do while he's here?"

"Gets in around nine. After his shift ends at eight." Finn put a tall glass under a spout and filled it with beer. "Orders dinner. Eats. Usually leaves with a woman. Rarely the same one."

Sounded like one of Waylon's Friday nights.

"Or I should say he used to leave with someone," Finn said.

"What do you mean used to?" Hannah asked.

"He stared eating alone and leaving alone."

Waylon scratched his chin. "When did the change start?"

"I don't know," the bartender said with a shrug. "Been a while. A few months back I guess. Maybe in August."

When Amber Reyes came back to town for her father's funeral. "And he only comes in on Thursdays?"

"Yep. Like clockwork."

"What about last Thursday?" Hannah asked. "Was he by himself?"

Finn laughed and set the beer down in front of a customer. "Nah, he wasn't alone. A hot redhead came in as he was finishing dinner. She was draped all over him, coming on strong."

"And how did he respond?" Waylon asked.

"Oh, he was into it. Feeling her up, stroking her leg. Smiling at her. Looked like those two were ready to get a room."

Hannah narrowed her eyes. "Really?"

That was the same question on Waylon's lips. The footage at Pandora's had showed a different sort of interplay in which Monty wasn't a happy camper. Maybe something had soured between them by the time they got to her place.

"Yeah," Finn said. "I guess he was looking for some action the other night and she was ready to show him a good time."

Hannah turned in a slow circle, scanning the place before looking back at the bartender. "We'd like to see the security footage from that night."

Finn ran a hand through his greasy-looking hair. "I wish I could show it to you, but we've been having problems with the system. It's on the fritz."

"That's convenient." Waylon exchanged a furtive glance with Hannah. "How about the cameras outside? Those aren't working either?"

After a moment of hesitation, Finn shook his head. "Nope. The whole system is down." He rubbed the back of his neck.

"Let me show you something." Waylon beckoned to him with a finger. The guy leaned across the bar and Waylon pointed to one of the cameras. "You see that little green light at the bottom? That says different. Tells us the cameras are operational and that you're lying."

The question was why.

Finn reeled back. "Nah. I'm not lying. You misunderstood me. They're working now. But they weren't Thursday."

Hannah raised an eyebrow. "Just got them fixed?"

"Yep. Sure did. Friday."

"Do you have a work order? A receipt?" Waylon folded his arms across his chest. "What company repaired the system?"

"My cousin fixed it," Finn said, easily. "He tinkers with electrical stuff. Really handy."

Hannah smiled. "If you're not lying, then you won't have any problem taking us to the office and showing us the footage that doesn't exist. Come on, sport." She hiked a thumb toward the hall.

"I've got customers. I can't just leave the bar and register unattended."

"Get moving," Waylon said. "Or I'll get you moving."

Hannah grimaced at the bartender. "Trust me, you don't want that."

"All right." Finn wiped his hands on a dish towel and led the way to the office in the back. He sat down behind a desk and logged into the computer.

Waylon and Hannah stood on either side of him, peering over his shoulder at the screen. He toggled over to the folder for the indoor cameras. Clicked one labeled Main Bar. Then December.

Footage for Thursday, December 5, was missing.

"Get up." Hannah tugged on his collar and the guy moved, letting her sit down. She got out of that folder and went to the recycle bin—a temporary storage location for items recently deleted, whether by mistake or purposefully. People often forgot to clear it.

The recycle bin was empty.

Her shoulders tensed but her face was deadpan.

Finn grinned. "See. I told you. This proves I wasn't lying."

Waylon shook his head. It was the exact opposite.

If the surveillance camera had been experiencing glitches, there would be footage that showed some problems throughout the day. Pieces missing. This proved the entire day had simply been deleted.

"Check the footage for the outside cameras," he said, and Finn stiffened, his premature smile falling from his face.

Hannah moved the mouse, sliding the cursor to the folder for the outside cameras. There were two. He pointed to the one that he thought offered the best view of the parking lot. She opened it and went to the night in question.

There was footage available. Waylon smiled.

Finn didn't move a step, but his gaze kept flying to the door like he wanted to run.

Waylon pinned him with a look and pointed a finger at him. "I hope you're not thinking of going anywhere."

"I'm just worried about my customers, that's all."

Hannah brought up the footage, sped to the point where Monty arrived and parked.

Shortly before ten a red Alfa Romeo Stelvio pulled into the lot. Pandora hopped out of her sporty SUV, wearing a short dress, leather boots and a fur jacket. The young woman put on lipstick and fluffed her hair before strutting inside the bar.

Carefully easing the footage forward, Hannah took the video to three minutes after ten. She let it play.

Waylon leaned in and watched alongside her.

Minutes later, Pandora sauntered out alone. She sashayed over to her vehicle and leaned against the hood, waiting. It wasn't long, a few seconds, until Monty left the bar, too. With his hands stuffed in his pockets, he strode up to her. He nodded as he said something.

A bright smile spread across Pandora's face. She stepped closer and ran her hand up his chest, but he backed away, ending the physical contact, and got in his truck. She pulled out of the lot first and he followed behind her.

Hannah sighed, her disappointment palpable.

This didn't confirm Finn's version of events. It also didn't prove that they weren't romantically involved either.

"Why did you lie about the security cameras glitching?" Waylon asked Finn.

"I don't know what you're talking about." The guy rubbed his arm, his gaze shifting. "There was no footage inside the bar. I guess I got it wrong about outside."

"The redhead who was in here the other night is dead. This is a murder investigation, understand?" Waylon stalked over to him, and Finn's eyes grew big as hubcaps. "I'm going to give you a choice. You can give us honest answers and we'll leave you alone. Or we get one of our techies in here and it'll be easy enough to prove you deleted the file. That's obstruction of justice, buddy. Continue to lie and it'll only make this worse. Also, it'll just tick me off. Means I'm going haul you in. Did you know you could get up to a year in jail?"

Hannah stood and went around the desk. "And because we don't appreciate having our time wasted, this place is going to be raided, regularly. We'll be sure to use a narcotics detection canine."

"So, I'm going to ask you one more time." Waylon got up close and had to peer down in his face since the bartender was a head shorter than him. "Why did you lie?"

Finn's gaze fell for a long a moment, then he looked back up at them. A fixed gleam in his eyes. "I didn't lie. Monty was hot and heavy with that woman."

"Lied about deleting the footage," Delaney said, clarifying for him. "*That woman* is dead, remember?"

"Sorry she's dead but it's not my fault," Finn snapped.

"Watch your tone." Waylon pointed a finger at him. "That's no way to talk to a lady."

"Thanks. But I'm no lady. I'm a detective."

A thought occurred to Waylon. "Maybe you deleted the video footage because it shows you slipping a roofie into Monty's drink. Maybe the redhead paid you to do it. Maybe you were in cahoots together and now that she's dead you're worried we'll think you killed her."

Finn's eyes grew big and he shook his head. "No. No way."

Hannah's face hardened. "Are you sure? If we find out that you're lying, you're going to regret it."

"I'm sure. It wouldn't have worked anyway. No way to slip

him a roofie. Monty only orders bottled beer while sitting at the bar. Always wants to open it himself. Never leaves his drink unattended. He'll chug it before going to the bathroom."

Sounded paranoid. But with everything going on, maybe the man had justified cause. If he was so cautious, it begged the question of whether he was indeed roofied or took the drug himself to cast reasonable doubt. "What about the redhead, was she ever in here before?"

"I'd never seen in here until last Thursday."

How did Pandora know to find Monty at the Howling Wolf on Thursday night at the right time?

"The file. Why did you really erase it?" Hannah demanded.

"I deleted the file because it was useless from going in and out. Real glitchy. You couldn't see anything. I've only got so much storage space on the drive. It made sense to get rid of it."

That was his *story,* and he was sticking to it for now.

"If something comes back to you and you remember things differently, let us know." Waylon handed him a business card, itching to take another go at this guy. But not now. Later, when they had more information. Use a lot more pressure and put the fear of God in the man.

Finn snatched the card. "Sure. I'll do that."

They went back out through the bar and left.

After they got in his truck, Hannah turned to him. "What do you make of it?"

"He's lying. About deleting the file for certain. Not so sure about his replay of how things went between Monty and Pandora inside the bar, though."

"I agree about the footage." Hannah nodded. "But do you still think Monty was sleeping with Pandora?"

He gave a one-shoulder shrug. The more he learned, the more he suspected Monty might not be guilty of murder. Didn't mean he wasn't sleeping with her. "I wouldn't put it past him." Monty was selfish, arrogant and tended to take what he wanted. "Do you have any idea what that ranch is worth with the cattle and access to the river?"

"No idea."

"Millions. Tens of millions. I've known men who have slept with two women at the same time for a heck of a lot less. And if he was bedding both of them, it would explain why he'd want it to keep it secret. So it doesn't upset the one who is still alive. He had to be extremely careful with Amber, didn't he? I mean with the engagement falling through ten years ago. Him using her to get the land way back then and now once again."

"I don't think it's that straightforward. He lied to her and proposed to get the land, but I think he's always truly cared about her. Monty isn't a typical user. He's not a womanizing manipulator. Not the way you want to believe."

The whole town had heard about the engagement. Two powerful, wealthy families about to be united. Then Amber Reyes fled in the night. Never to be seen again until her father's funeral. Waylon had no idea why it had fallen apart.

Or that Monty had lied, seduced her and proposed only to get the land for his family. It simply had been a connect-the-dots suspicion of his.

But thanks to Hannah Delaney's little slipup, he knew for certain now.

His phone rang. "It's the medical examiner." He put it on the Bluetooth speaker in the truck. "Hey, Roger. Delaney is with me. What do you have for us?"

"You'll have my full report in the morning, but I wanted to give you a quick update. I've narrowed the time of death to between six and seven in the morning. And she didn't die from exsanguination. The victim was strangled to death first. The perp waited before slitting her throat. Based on the low amount of blood flow I'd estimate twenty minutes."

"Maybe he was busy setting the scene," Hannah said, "and

saved cutting her throat for last to keep from tracking blood around."

"I was thinking the same possibility. Anything else, Roger?"

"The victim recently had intercourse. My guess is fairly close to the time of death."

"Consensual," Hannah said, "not rape, right, Doc?"

"Yes. But he didn't leave behind any bodily fluids. That's about it. Wanted you to know straight away. The rest will be in my report."

"Thanks, Roger." Waylon disconnected. "We need more answers. Fiona Frye is supposed to come at nine. Something she said keeps bothering me."

"About the proof that Pandora was seeing Monty?"

"No, not that, but it is odd. Right? I mean if she was seeing Monty or someone she trusted, why would she need insurance? The part that bugs me is when she told us her daughter was waiting until things were 'official' before she could tell anyone." The word kept turning over in his head.

"Like a deal for the land?"

Rubbing his eyes, Waylon fought a yawn. "Maybe. There's a whole lot about this case that I don't like." Things niggling at the back of his mind. "A puzzle with too many missing pieces." He started the engine. "Too many things just don't add up. The missing micro SD card in the security camera at Pandora's. The techies cracked into her hub and everything before that night was deleted. Her entire place was wiped clean of prints, except for the studio where she and Monty were found. The ketamine in his system. This story from the bartender about deleting a bad file to save on storage space. Now no bodily fluids left in the victim."

"What's odd about the last part Roger told us?"

He pulled out of the lot and hit the road. "There were no used condoms found in her home. If Monty slept with her, he didn't run out to dispose of it, only to go back, drug himself and wait to be found. Whoever she did sleep with right before she was murdered was careful." Waylon shook his head. "We can't discount what the bartender told us either about Monty and Pandora getting hot and heavy in the bar. What reason would he have to make up something like that?"

Delaney sighed.

A similar frustration pounded in Waylon's temples. "It's time Monty filled in some of the blanks for us. Talking to him after we speak to Ms. Frye would be best. Can you arrange for him to come in, with his lawyer if he insists, for a chat at eleven?" Plenty of time. There shouldn't be any excuses.

"Sure." She took out her cell and fired off a text. "I'll follow up with a phone call and convince him it's in his best interest to cooperate and simply talk to us already. Stonewalling is not helping him."

Although Waylon was starting to suspect that Monty wasn't the murderer, he still expected the eldest Powell son to be tight-lipped and lawyered up.

Sometimes he had to rattle a cage and poke the bear, get it angry to get progress. And one thing he knew about Montgomery Powell was that when he was angry, he ranted, at times even saying things that he shouldn't.

Tomorrow, Waylon would see if it'd work.

Chapter Twelve

The text message was unexpected.

Tapping her fingernails on her desk, Valentina wasn't sure what to do with the news she had just received. Tying up loose ends was always a good thing. But there was a bigger opportunity here. She simply had to see how to use it.

A knock on her office door pulled her from her thoughts. "Enter."

Max and Leo shuffled inside the room. From their hung heads and wary expressions, they'd failed.

Valentina crossed her legs and leaned back in her chair. "I'm going to ask you something, Leo, in a way that you can understand. What is the maximum effective range of an excuse?" The US Army was fond of that question, or so Roman had told her when she hired Leo. Back then she'd seen such potential in the young man, to prove himself, rise through the ranks of her drug empire. Staring at him now, she was no longer so sure. If he couldn't kill one man, how could he be trusted with the inner workings of the cartel?

"Zero meters is the maximum effective range of an excuse, ma'am," Leo said, hands clasped behind his back, standing at attention.

"Remember that and think carefully before you answer my next question. Why isn't Holden Powell dead?"

He looked up at her. "The family was finally out in the open at the tree lighting ceremony in the center of town. I had him in my sights. But he was holding a baby the entire time and had his pregnant wife next to him."

Valentina wrinkled her brow. "I'm not hearing a reason."

Confusion took over Leo's face. "I couldn't get a clear, clean shot. He—he had a baby in his arms."

"I understood the words the first time."

Anger sparked in his eyes. "I could've hit the kid by accident. If I took a head shot, the child would've fallen. Might've cracked his skull on the pavement. They're fragile as eggs when they're that little. Did you want me to hurt a baby?"

Her thoughts careened to Julian. His laughter. His smile. His warmth. "No. I only wanted the brother dead. Him first. The one with a kid." Like her own brother, who had to leave his son fatherless.

Because of Montgomery Powell.

Seemed fair.

"First, ma'am? Who would you like me to kill second?"

"Buck," she said, the name spilling from her lips with bitterness. "The leader of that clan. But I want the dominoes to fall in the proper order until I've destroyed everything Montgomery holds dear. Not that you've proven yourself capable of helping me." She slid her gaze to her burly guard. "And what did you do, Max? Simply stand there and watch this failure unfold?"

"No, *jefa*. Leo asked me to stir up the crowd. That way after there were gunshots, it would appear random. Unplanned. In-the-heat-of-the-moment kind of thing and not like an assassination."

She hadn't considered that. "Smart. Still doesn't change the fact that an opportunity was wasted."

Leo dared to step forward. "But it wasn't, ma'am," he said, his voice rippling with confidence.

Maybe she wouldn't kill him today if he redeemed himself. "Explain."

"After the gunshots, Montgomery Powell picked up a woman and rushed her to a vehicle. The entire family raced to the hospital. We followed them over. I slipped inside and hung around in the waiting room, eavesdropping. The woman, Amber Reyes, is pregnant. And the baby is Monty's. It's going to be a boy. They were all overjoyed."

A sweet smile spread across her face. Now she knew precisely what to do with the information she'd received in the text message. "There's something I want you both to do."

Leo straightened. "Anything, ma'am."

She grabbed a notepad, pen and the folder from her top desk drawer. "First, I want you to go to this address." She copied it from the text that had been sent to her. "You'll find a dead body in the house. I want you to take it and put it in the trunk of another vehicle." She wrote down the second address, along with the make, model and license of the car. "Stealth will be required. People will be at home and asleep at the second house." She handed him the paper. "You're not to be noticed."

"That's it?" Leo asked. "You don't want me to kill anyone?"

"Well, I did, but you messed that up, didn't you? For this task, the blood has already been spilled. Get this errand right. No mistakes."

Both Leo and Max nodded.

"You may go." She waved them out, picked up her phone and dialed Officer Nicholas Foley.

He answered on the fourth ring. "Yes, ma'am. The Laramie PD has the cell phone that was *found* in Montgomery's locker."

"Good boy," she said, like he was a dog. "I have another mission for you. Tomorrow morning, I need you to do your job and make a traffic stop."

"Who am I pulling over?" he asked.

"Amber Reyes. She lives on the big ranch on Longhorn River Road. She will have an appointment in town at ten. There's only one route for her to take. Expect her to leave her home sometime between nine fifteen and nine thirty. She likes to arrive early. During the traffic stop, you need to search her trunk."

"Want to tell me what I'm looking for?"

Valentina grinned. "Don't you like surprises?"

"No, ma'am. Not when I'm working for you."

She chuckled. "Once the trunk is open it'll be obvious. Trust me on that."

"Are you sure she'll be going that way around that time? I can't sit out on the road forever. Someone will notice me. This appointment is set, and she'll keep it?"

"No, not yet. But if you pass the phone to your wife, she can help me arrange that part."

"Sure. One second."

There was a rustling sound. "Hello, Ms. Sandoval. What do you need from me?" the wife asked.

"Two things. Both are equally important. Contact Amber Reyes. Set up some kind of urgent meeting in the morning somewhere in town. Tell her she needs to be there by ten. You will not accept 'no' for answer. Ensure Ms. Reyes is in the right place at the right time."

"What else?"

"The project you worked on regarding Holly Powell. Activate it as soon as possible."

"I could reach out to Erica Egan tonight. Get the ball rolling. That woman will answer the phone no matter what time it is. But she'll want the proof tonight as well. Or would you like me to wait until tomorrow morning?"

"Which one is as soon as possible? Tonight? Or tomorrow?"

"Okay. I understand. I'll call her right now and arrange everything tonight. You should see it on the news about Holly before lunch."

Valentina ended the call.

Never underestimate the power of an inside man. Or woman.

Chapter Thirteen

The next morning, Amber stared absently through the windshield of her Jeep, feeling unsettled as she drove into town. Vera, Holly's secretary, had called, insisting that she come down to the mayor's office by nine. To talk with Holly away from the house in private.

She cringed on the inside over how that discussion was going to go.

Hold your ground. Create boundaries. It'll be fine.

She'd already decided there would be no talk of marriage or the status of her relationship with Monty at all. Baby talk was fine. Nothing more.

The one bright spot was that Vera promised to have a wide selection of munchies from Divine Treats. A boiled egg, applesauce and toast for a quick breakfast wouldn't hold her long. She was ready for a mouthwatering, sugary treat. Then she crossed her fingers her appetite would last.

She took a sip from the new water bottle Holly had gotten Buck to purchase last night. Already it had made a huge difference in her water consumption. Monty's family was overbearing and intrusive, but they meant well and looked out for those in their inner circle.

Rubbing her belly, with one hand on the steering wheel, she thought she'd be overjoyed to know that Monty loved her, to have proof she mattered more than the land and the river. And a big part of her was, but the only way to know for sure was to let him lose it all.

The idea of taking away the ranch, the land, generations of hard work from him, from her unborn son, from Kayce, from the child Grace was carrying now, made her heart weep.

As much as Monty didn't want to admit it, he was born to be a rancher. One day he'd come to realize it. But she couldn't let that happen with him working on someone else's land.

The next generation of Powells being born might have a love for ranching in their souls. Wouldn't that be something? The operation was large enough to share among so many, especially once it was combined with the Reyes land, and Matt was expanding the business further. Offering wild game hunting for tourists. Cabins were being built on the Little Shooting Star. She'd heard all the boys had pitched in, helping to build the cabins that would be rented out.

She made a right onto Route 207, which turned into Third Street, the main road into town.

Who was she to steal such a thing from everyone just to be 100 percent positive Monty's feelings for her were real? That she mattered more?

In the end, would he resent her? Would her son, after he learned about the incredible legacy that should've been passed to him?

A siren whooped once behind her.

Amber looked up in the rearview mirror. Red and blue lights flashed on a state police cruiser. Sighing, she pulled over, came to a stop and put the SUV in Park.

An officer strolled up to the driver's side and gestured for her to roll down the window with a gloved hand.

"I'm sorry, Officer. Was I speeding?" She had a tendency to do that. A bad habit she needed to break.

No more speeding with baby on board.

"License and registration." A rough voice rumbled in that authoritative way cops had. He hooked his thumbs on his utility belt and waited.

"Oh." She reached over to her glove compartment. Found the registration and handed it to him.

"License."

She opened her purse and stared at the envelope she still hadn't opened. Her father's letter. Bypassing it, she grabbed her wallet and gave him her license. "I know I was going too fast. If you let me off with a warning, I promise not to do it anymore."

He looked over her documentation. "Your registration from Texas expired last month."

She cringed. "My father died in August. I came here for his funeral and after the reading of his will things got topsy-turvy. I wasn't expecting to stay this long, but then I did. I didn't forward my mail and didn't realize the expiration was coming up. Once my brother pointed out to me that it had in fact expired, I didn't know if I should renew the registration in Texas or get a new one here. Everything in my life is changing so fast. It's so complicated and messy. I might stay. I might go. But I'll know for sure in a couple of weeks and figured I would take care of it then. In January. Once I knew if I was getting married or not. Or staying here. Or going back to Texas. Do you see what I'm saying?"

The cop grimaced.

"That was long-winded. I apologize…" She looked at his name tag. "Officer Foley." She looked over his state police uniform and made the connection. "Do you know Monty Powell? You two probably work together. We're very close."

"Ma'am, please step out of the vehicle."

"Come again?"

He put his hand on the hilt of his weapon. "Please step out of the vehicle."

She stiffened. "Yes, Officer." She did as he instructed, and her legs shook. Something like this had never happened to her before. Sure, she'd gotten a ticket before. Okay, lots of speeding tickets, but the police had never asked her to get out like she was a criminal.

He peered inside her vehicle and looked around. "Ma'am, please open your trunk."

"Is this really necessary?" she asked, incredulously. A bit excessive, wasn't it?

His features tightened to stone. His jaw set as he put his hand back on the hilt of his gun.

A flutter zipped through her chest. "Of course." Amber tapped her coat pocket, checking to make sure the key fob was inside, raised her palms and walked around to the rear of the Jeep. "This seems silly, if you ask me. I only have an emergency kit in there. Flares. Jumper cables. And a spare tire." Since the key fob was on her, she just moved her foot under the rear bumper in a straight kicking motion, activating the hands-free sensor.

The hazard lights flashed and the liftgate opened.

Her heart dropped to her stomach and the ground beneath her feet seemed to crumble away like the earth had split open wide. She staggered back. "No," she choked out.

Fiona Frye was dead. In her trunk.

"Ma'am, put your hands on your head. You're under arrest." The officer wrenched her wrists behind her back and slapped handcuffs on her while reciting her Miranda rights. He steered her to his vehicle and put a hand on the top of her head, helping her inside.

Her pulse was pounding a mile of minute, but a weird calm

stole over her. "Can you please grab my purse and water bottle? I'm pregnant. The doctor said I had to stay hydrated."

The officer hesitated a second. "Sure. But you've got to wait until after you're booked to get the water bottle."

"Can I be booked at the sheriff's department?" she asked. The sheriff was in California helping his and Grace's mother with something, leaving Holden in charge.

Holden would sort this out. She'd be okay there.

At the Laramie Police Department, with Waylon Wright eager to believe in this dreadful conspiracy spreading like a disease, there was no telling what would happen to her.

"I do know Monty, ma'am," the officer said. "His brother is chief deputy at the sheriff's. Sorry, but I'll be taking you to LPD." He slammed the door shut.

Oh, my God. Fiona, the next person who stood to inherit the land, was dead, and she was about to be booked for her murder. If she hadn't been sitting, she would've collapsed.

First Monty.

Now her.

Who would be the next person to die? And who would be blamed?

Chapter Fourteen

Done prepping for his upcoming interview with Monty, Waylon closed the folder he planned to bring inside the room with him. He couldn't believe what they'd found on Monty's flip phone that had been seized from his work locker.

Montgomery Powell had a lot of explaining to do, and Hannah Delaney wasn't going to be there to help him. When Fiona Frye never showed up for their appointment, he'd sent her to go check on Ms. Frye and to take another crack at questioning Pandora's neighbors. Neither who lived on either side of the young woman had been at home when they'd tried before. They could get lucky. A neighbor might have seen Pandora with Monty or with some other man.

"Hey, Wright." One of the officers who had participated in the execution of the search warrant last night came over to him. "Maybe we searched the wrong ranch last night?"

He sipped his coffee. "What are you talking about?"

"I guess you haven't heard. Amber Reyes was just booked for the murder of Fiona Frye and is sitting in a holding cell right now."

That caught his attention. "Do you mean for the murder of Pandora Frye?" he asked, but that still didn't make a lick of sense. Instinct told him that she wasn't a murderer. Besides, based on the security camera footage, she wasn't guilty.

"No. The mother. Fiona Frye."

His gut twisted. Waylon shot him a confused look. "Who was the arresting officer?"

"A guy with the state police. He's still here doing the paperwork." The cop pointed to him.

Familiar face. "Thanks," Waylon said to the cop. Grabbing the folder for his interview, he got out of his chair and waltzed over to the state trooper. "Officer Foley. Two times in two days that you're here. First, you dropped off the phone from Powell's locker."

"Yeah, they figured it made sense for me to run it by since I live in the area."

"What brings you here today?"

"Routine traffic stop turned into something more. There was a dead body in the trunk."

In mock surprise, Waylon raised both brows. "Wow, you don't see that every day. Especially not around here in our small town."

Foley flashed an easy smile. "I know, right?"

Waylon sat on the edge of the desk the guy was using. "Walk me through how it happened. The specifics."

"I was on my way to work when my wife called. So I pulled over to see what the Mrs. needed."

"Where were you?"

"Oh, I was on Route 207 near the intersection of Longhorn River Road. Anyway, this woman—"

"Name?"

"Amber Reyes. She failed to come to a complete stop at the intersection where there was a red light and didn't use her signal when you make a right turn. Turns out her registration has been expired for weeks. Then she started rambling incoherently. I asked her to step out of the vehicle. She didn't want to do it. Tried to talk her way out of it, still not making any sense. I got a weird feeling, you know, a cop's sixth sense," he said, and Waylon nodded. "With all those violations and how suspicious she was acting. So I asked to see the inside of her trunk. Bingo! Dead body."

"Golly. That's some story." A lot of stories were flying around lately. Waylon stood. "Hey, tell me something. Where do you live?"

Foley spouted out his address. The trooper lived on the western outskirts of town while the Reyes ranch was in the northeast, nowhere near town.

"Huh? That's clear on the other side. Do you drive past Longhorn River Road every day?"

"No. I was craving one of those Cronuts from Divine Treats and decided to take the scenic route to enjoy it on the drive. Pure coincidence what happened."

"Yeah, three things I love. Scenic routes. Perfect timing. And coincidence." Waylon clapped the trooper on the back. "You keep up the fine work."

Foley's smile brightened. "Will do, sir."

Waylon made his way back to the holding cells, where he found Amber Reyes looking pale, rigid and unwell. "Ms. Reyes."

She met his gaze with tired eyes. "Detective Wright. Are you here to gloat?"

"No, ma'am. I admit I'm guilty of schadenfreude when it comes to the Powells, but please believe that I take no enjoyment from the troubles of anyone else outside that family. Especially when it involves another murder."

"I didn't do it. I don't know how Fiona's body got into the trunk of my car."

"You're entitled to have a lawyer present."

"They told me I had to wait to make my phone call. But I'd tell you the same thing with an attorney present. I didn't like Fiona or Pandora. But I didn't hate either woman. I didn't wish them ill. I certainly didn't kill them."

He believed her. "Speaking of ill, that's how you look. Can I get you anything?"

"The officer who arrested me brought my water bottle and my purse. Can I have them and something to eat?" She put a hand to her stomach and rubbed it. It almost seemed an unconscious movement. "I had to go the ER last night. The doctor said I need to stay hydrated and eat. I missed breakfast."

The way she sat, hunched like the weight of the world rested on her shoulders, highlighted the outline of her belly bump. "Are you pregnant?"

Her eyes widened, but she nodded.

"Is it Monty's?"

She licked her lips and bit the inside of her cheek. "Yes."

"I'll make sure you get your phone call, the water bottle and something to eat. I can't give you your purse. Was there something inside you wanted?" Maybe she had prenatal vitamins or something for nausea.

"There's a sealed letter. From my father. I think I'm finally ready to read it."

"I'll get you taken care of, ma'am." He turned to leave, but then looked back at her. "Don't worry, Ms. Reyes. You won't be in here long. Just be patient. I don't think you killed Fiona Frye any more than you did Pandora."

"As you've already pointed out, I stand to gain if those two are gone. Why do you think I'm innocent?"

"Because I don't believe in coincidence. No such thing. And when people start using it to explain something that doesn't add up, it sets my teeth on edge. I'm going to get to the bottom of this. You can trust that."

On his way to the interrogation rooms, another officer stopped him.

"Montgomery Powell is in room one with his lawyer waiting for you."

"Thanks. Do me a favor. Ms. Reyes is in holding. Let her make her phone call ASAP. Also, see that she gets plenty of water, let her order whatever she wants to eat from Delgado's Bar and Grill—I'll cover the charge—and find her purse. There's a sealed envelope inside. Supposedly a letter. Check it to be sure and then let her have it."

"No problem."

Waylon went to room one and grabbed the handle. Taking a breath, he considered how to play this. *Poke the bear or good cop?*

Today felt like the perfect day to rattle a cage. "Poke the bear it is," he whispered to himself.

He entered the room and sat down.

Across the metal table was Monty, wearing a button-down under his shearling jacket, jeans and his black cowboy hat. His lawyer sat stiff as a board in a suit, sipping a coffee.

Waylon slapped the folder down and put his hand on top of it. "I see someone has already offered you something to drink."

"Let's get on with it," Monty said.

"I'm Tim Lemke, Mr. Powell's attorney. He has graciously agreed to cooperate with you today. We only ask that you be respectful of his time."

"Certainly." Waylon nodded. "Walk me through the events of Thursday evening."

Monty opened his mouth, but Lemke put a hand on his forearm, stopping him.

"Could you please be more specific?" the attorney asked.

"Sure." Waylon shrugged. "Where were you at nine p.m. on Thursday night?"

"The Howling Wolf Roadhouse. I have dinner there—"

Lemke leaned over to his client. "Only answer the question asked. Don't offer any additional information."

"Look," Waylon said, "this will take all day unless he fills in the blanks by offering additional information, which is the reason he's here. I thought you wanted me to be respectful of his time. Either you killed Pandora Frye or you didn't. So, if you want to get on with it, start talking."

"I have dinner there on Thursdays," Monty said.

"Why Thursdays?" Waylon wondered. "Why not Fridays?"

"I have seniority. I only work Monday through Thursday. That's my Friday, the night I want to unwind. The other three days I spend working on the ranch. Long, hard hours and I don't feel like driving to a bar afterward."

Satisfied, Waylon nodded. "Do you only eat dinner there? Do you ever pick up women?"

Monty clenched his jaw. "I used to."

"What changed?"

Monty looked at his attorney.

"I don't see the relevance," Lemke said. "How does this pertain to last Thursday? Why don't we stick to that?"

Everyone had secrets, the guilty and innocent alike. But Waylon needed to know why Monty wanted to hide his relationship with Amber if he wasn't sleeping with Pandora.

"Okay. Did you see and speak with Pandora Frye at the Howling Wolf that evening?" Waylon asked.

"I did."

"And?"

Monty looked to his attorney and got the okay before going on. "She approached me as I was finishing dinner."

"Did she make any amorous overtures that you welcomed or encouraged?"

"She tried to touch me a couple of times. Pandora is— *was*—a handsy person. I didn't take it as her hitting on me or anything, but I also let her know that I didn't like it."

"Let her know how?"

"I removed her hands from my body."

"Interesting. The bartender at the Howling Wolf, Finn, told us that you two were all over each other and looked like you—and I quote—'needed to get a room.' Any idea why he would tell us that if it wasn't true?"

"None at all. I think you should go back and ask him again."

That was on Waylon's list of things to do for this afternoon. They needed to squeeze the bartender and get to the bottom of why his story felt off. "Why did Pandora approach you?"

"Told me she didn't think Amber was going to marry me. But once Pandora inherited the land, that we could strike a deal where I could get it."

"What were the terms of this deal?"

"She refused to talk about it at the Howling Wolf. Told me that I had to do it at her place over a drink or there would be no deal. Then she left."

"What happened next?"

"I paid the bill. Went outside to find her waiting. I agreed since I didn't see the harm in hearing what she had to say."

"You drove yourself to her place?"

Monty nodded. "I followed her over. She let me in and showed me into her studio, where she worked. I took a seat. She poured me a drink. Then she made small talk for a bit. The conversation turned to Amber and Chance. Pandora told me that she would never give up the Reyes family home, but she didn't want that to put her at odds with her half siblings. She wanted to get to know them. And then." He shook his head. "I don't remember anything clearly until I woke up in the hospital."

"Did you watch Pandora pour your drink?"

Lowering his head, Monty looked like he was thinking about it. "No. She handed me one of her portfolio books and asked me what I thought of her work while she poured the drinks."

Maybe he had let his guard down around her. What danger would he have assumed a woman weighing one hundred twenty pounds would've posed to him? How was he supposed to know where the night was headed?

One possible theory.

But there were others and they all needed to be explored. "The portion of the Reyes land that might've gone to Pandora is extremely valuable to your family, isn't it?"

"It is."

"Valuable enough for you to have started a romantic relationship with Pandora. To have seduced her. Perhaps promised marriage to her."

Monty's eyes hardened. "No."

"That's impossible?" Waylon gave a light, incredulous chuckle. "You wouldn't seduce a woman for the land? Or should I say once more. The way you seduced a young and vulnerable Amber Reyes when she was only nineteen years old shortly after losing her mother."

"Watch it," Monty said, through gritted teeth.

"Did I strike a nerve?" *Good.* Waylon was only getting started. "In your locker at work, a burner phone was found. I printed out screenshots of some of the texts." He pulled a couple of sheets from the folder and slid them across the table.

Monty picked up the papers. He and his lawyer read through them. Alarm washed over Monty's face.

"Steamy stuff in there," Waylon said. "Kinky, too. A lot of talk about what you liked and how much she enjoyed giving it to you. How much she loved you. How she couldn't wait to marry you."

"I've never seen these texts." Monty finally looked scared. "I didn't write them or receive them."

"My client's name is never mentioned," Lemke said, stabbing the paper. "Nor that of Ms. Frye. Only McDreamy, Lover, Bubba and Cupcake. These texts could be between any two people."

Waylon frowned. "The problem is that the phone was found in your client's locker and the number he texted did in fact belong to Pandora Frye. There were also some racy photos that you took of Pandora that were found on the phone." He took blown-up copies of the pictures from the folder and slid those over next.

Monty peered down at them and his jaw dropped.

"Looks like you're into bondage," Waylon said, his stomach turning. That was not his thing. "And asphyxiation during sex." There were photos of Pandora tied up, nude, someone with a gloved hand choking her. The person had worn long sleeves. In some of the photos pleasure was on her face, either real or feigned. But in the rest the fear in her eyes was clear. All the pictures and texts were from last month. "Maybe you got too rough during sex on Thursday night. Choked her to death by accident." Most crimes of passion were violent, such as strangulation or a stabbing, a hands-on act done in the heat of the moment. "Then you got desperate and needed to cover it up." He shoved a picture of Pandora, lying on the floor, naked and murdered, in his face.

"Go to hell!" Monty threw the photos at him and jumped to his feet. "We're done here!"

"You're going to sit back down," Waylon said calmly.

Monty narrowed his eyes and clenched his hands. "Or else what?"

"Or else I'm going to have a little chat with Amber Reyes. Who, by the way, is sitting in a holding cell right now because a dead body was found in her trunk this morning."

"What?" Monty reeled back. "Whose body?" he demanded.

But Waylon was on a roll and ignored the question. "And when I talk to the mother of your unborn child, I'm going to show her those racy photos and tell her my theory about your kinky side."

A ferocious expression darkened Monty's face, and he cocked back his fist, ready to pound into Waylon.

His attorney jumped between him and the table. "Don't do it. You can't."

"No, let him," Waylon said with a grin. Gone were their high school days where he'd been smaller than Monty. Now he was two inches taller, outweighed him by about twenty pounds of solid muscle and still had sharp reflexes. He could've stopped him if he wanted, but he welcomed the punch. "I'd love to charge him with assault of a police officer. I can put you in a cell next to Amber's."

"You sick son of a—"

"Stop and get control of yourself," his lawyer warned. "This is what he wants. You acting like a crazed animal with anger management issues." The lawyer faced Waylon. "My client's face was not in any of the photos. You can't prove it was him."

"The phone they found isn't mine," Monty said.

"Then how did it get in your locker?"

"I don't know, but the only reason you're doing this is because of what happened in high school." Monty lowered his fist. "I'm sorry, okay? I didn't know Tara was your girlfriend when I asked her to homecoming."

This wasn't about some gripe from high school, but since Monty had brought it up, he was willing to discuss it. "I told you she was and that the only reason she said yes to you was because your father and hers were in business. That she thought she had to agree."

"And I thought you were a lying, sore loser! It wasn't until I didn't end up going to homecoming and she confessed to me that she was relieved not to go with me that I learned the truth."

"Take what you want, regardless of who gets hurt," Waylon said. "That's your motto. That's the code you live by. And as if that wasn't enough, you had to break my hand."

Indignation twisted Monty's features, reddening his cheeks

as he shook his head. "You picked a fight after football practice. I was holding my helmet and used it to block your fist. I didn't mean to break your hand and end your football season."

"I guess you didn't mean to throw me into the trophy display case either, shredding my face with glass." He had fallen face-first. Took thirty stitches. Not to mention the pain. For the rest of his senior year, everyone called him *Scarface*.

"It was an accident. I never intended for you to get hurt. Not like that. And I came to your home and apologized."

"Only because your father made you." The gall. Monty could've shoved that artificial, hollow apology where the sun didn't shine for all Waylon had cared. "What really burns me to the core is that after the stitches and getting a cast, I was the one sentenced to detention for fighting. Not you. Oh, no, a Powell was too good for detention. That was beneath the son of the almighty Buck and Holly."

A roar of angry laughter rolled out of Monty. "You're right, I didn't get detention because I'm a Powell. But what you don't know is that my father whipped me with a leather strap until I bled because you were smaller than me at that time and got hurt so badly. I didn't get to go to homecoming. I didn't get to finish the football season either. My father pulled me from the team. And I'm the one who had to pay for a new display case by working on the ranch well before dawn prior to school and after until midnight. Every day for months. He came down on me particularly hard because I was to be made the example for my brothers. The cautionary tale of what not to do. So, yeah, I'm sorry I didn't get two weeks of detention, but there was ranch justice exacted on your behalf. Take some consolation in that."

Waylon had no idea his father had been so harsh on him. If he had known, it would've been water under the bridge eons ago.

"No matter what you think of me," Monty said, "I'm not

a murderer and I have never slept with Pandora. And I won't tolerate you hurting Amber to get to me."

"Then why were you hiding your relationship with Amber?"

"It all looks bad! Having a relationship with her makes it look worse, especially if you think I was sleeping with Pandora, too. But I wasn't and never would."

Waylon spotted another opening and pushed. "Why *never*? Why such an impossibility? She was a very pretty girl and you had a lot to gain by doing so."

"Sleeping with Pandora Frye, hell, looking at her the wrong way would have hurt Amber. I broke her heart once. I love her. I want to win her back. Last night I told her the land doesn't matter. We can wait to get married to prove it to her. Fiona Frye can have it for all I care. Even if it means my family's legacy has to die. Amber, our baby, that's all that matters."

Waylon leaned back in his chair. "The dead body in Amber's trunk was Fiona Frye."

Monty spit out a curse. "I don't believe this." Heaving a ragged breath, he scrubbed his face with his hands. "This can't be happening. Amber didn't do it. You probably figure the same. Why would she drive around with a dead body in the trunk? Unless you think I did it and asked her to take the body somewhere?"

"I don't think you did it." Waylon stood. "There's a bigger game at play here. I needed you to be honest. I'm talking bare-your-soul-in-a-confessional kind of honest to fill in some of the blanks. I need to get to the bottom of this before any more dead bodies turn up. No hard feelings. Right?"

"To clarify," Lemke said, "you're not charging my client?"

Waylon took a deep cleansing breath. "No, I'm not charging him."

"You're going to release Amber?" Monty asked.

"She will be. There's a procedure. I need to talk to the chief and explain."

"I want to see her," Monty said. "Make sure she's all right. She needs to eat and drink water."

"I made sure she's being taken care of."

An urgent rap on the door interrupted them before a cop poked his head inside. "Assistant District Attorney Melanie Merritt is on the phone for you. Says it can't wait. You can pick up line two in the next room."

A tingle zipped down Waylon's spine. "I'll be right back." He hurried next door and answered the phone. "Howdy, darling, please tell me this call is of a personal nature."

Two and a half years ago, when Melanie moved to the area, before he knew she was going to be the new ADA, they'd run into each other at a bar in Wayward Bluffs. One thing had led to another, and they'd slept together.

Since then, they'd been in a quasi-relationship. Unofficially and under wraps. Always on her terms. They usually met at his place or hers three to four times a week. Sometimes in the middle of the day for a hot quickie. Strictly sex had become sentimental and even sweet. But he was ready to take things to the next level. Exclusivity in secret was no longer enough. He wanted to go from quasi to serious. Surprising her with tickets to the Caribbean for Christmas was either going to get him what he wanted or scare her off.

"Sorry to disappoint you, cowboy," she said, her tone all business, and the spark of anticipatory joy in him fizzled. "Next time watch it, I could've had you on speaker."

The line between personal and professional were critical to her. He got it and had to if he wanted to see her whenever she fancied herself in the mood.

"Are you not alone?" he asked.

"Yes and no. Someone unexpected is paying me a visit. I waited until he went to get coffee to call you because you tend to be unpredictable on the phone. I never know what filthy thing might come out of your mouth. I need to see you, Delaney and Montgomery Powell right now."

"Delaney is wrapped up at the moment, but I'm with Powell. I've got him in the next room."

"Good. I'm sure you've been scratching your head over the Pandora Frye case."

"As a matter of fact, I have. The pieces don't add up." He had the feeling Monty was being framed.

"I think I have some answers for you. Get him over to my office on the double. This can't wait for any reason." She hung up before he could respond.

"Yes, ma'am," he said to himself. He pulled out his phone and called Delaney. "Hey, Fiona Frye is dead."

"I figured as much. I'm at her place now. Looks like a tornado went through here."

"The body was found in Amber Reyes's vehicle."

"You've got to be kidding me."

"Wish I was. Hey, Monty claims he wasn't sleeping with Pandora and that their discussion at the bar was all business. Funny thing is, I believe him. Which means the bartender is lying. Go back and talk to him again. Find out why. Tell him we've got a witness who was in the bar that night contradicting his story. Lean hard on him."

"Are you mansplaining to me how to do my job, Lieutenant?"

Waylon cleared his throat. "Apologies. You've got this. I'm heading to the ADA's office with Monty."

"Why?"

"Don't know. She wants to see us about the case. I'll text you with an update when I know more."

"Okay." They hung up, and he ducked back into the interrogation room. "The ADA has information about this case. She needs to see us in her office immediately."

"But I need to see Amber."

"That'll have to wait. Trust me, she's fine." Waylon hurried Monty and his attorney out of the room and down the hall. "Hey, do you know a state trooper by the name of Foley?"

"Yeah. Nick."

"Does he have a grudge against you? Any reason to have it in for you?"

"None that I can think of. Why?"

Waylon shook his head, not ready to get into it any deeper. "Only wondering."

As they crossed through the bullpen, Detective Kent Kramer was ushering in Holly Powell in handcuffs. Her assistant, Eddie Something, was following them, carrying her purse.

"Mom!" Monty rushed over to her. "What's going on?"

"I've been arrested." She held up her hands, wrists cuffed in front of her.

"For what?" her son asked.

"Embezzlement."

The Powell family house of cards was tumbling down today. Waylon approached the other detective. "What's going on, Kent?"

"Erica Egan stopped by to see me earlier as a *courtesy* and handed over proof that Mrs. Powell has been embezzling money from the mayor's office. Twenty-five thousand dollars."

"That's absurd," Monty said. "She doesn't have a need to steal any money."

"I had Eddie call Buck to get our attorney, Corthell," Holly said.

"He's on the way, along with your husband." Eddie stepped forward. "I also asked Brianne to get out in front of this."

"Not Corthell, Mom." Monty shook his head. "You need a criminal attorney." He grabbed Lemke by the arm and shoved him toward his mother. "Use mine."

"Anyway," Kent said, "I think Egan was so generous sharing the information before she broke the story because she wanted to catch us arresting Mrs. Powell on camera. I'm sure it's all over the news by now."

"The world is going to hell in a handbasket, Mom," Monty said. "Amber was arrested, too."

"Oh no! That poor thing," Holly paled, pressing her hands to her chest. "Is she all right?"

"Have them put Mrs. Powell in the cell next to Ms. Reyes," Waylon said to Kent. "We need to go see the ADA. She said it can't wait for any reason." He took Monty by the arm, and the man jerked free of his grip. *Guess there are hard feelings.* "Let's go."

Chapter Fifteen

"What's this all about?" Monty asked, walking into the assistant district attorney's office. Best for them to get straight to it. The sooner they did, the sooner he could see Amber.

"Take a seat," Melanie Merritt said, seated behind her desk. She turned toward a man who was standing in the corner, staring out the window. "This is Agent Welliver. He's with the Drug Enforcement Agency. This is Montgomery Powell and Detective Lieutenant Waylon Wright." The ADA used Waylon's full pompous title that everyone else simply shortened to detective.

The man strolled over to the desk, holding a cup of coffee. Looked to be in his late fifties. Weathered. He wore a crisp black blazer and jeans. He offered a tight smile. "I'd say it's a pleasure to meet you, but I come as the bearer of bad news."

"Related to the homicide case of Pandora Frye?" Waylon asked.

Monty cut his gaze to the detective. He was still simmering over the interrogation but he now had a better understanding of Waylon and was trying to not take the harsh tactics so personally.

But it felt brutally personal.

"I believe so," Agent Welliver said. "We've been working on a case for a long time. Years really. Trying to bring down the Sandoval cartel. Earlier this year, we finally infiltrated them. Got our guy recruited. He's been working as a driver. Feeds us information."

"Some of that information helped us with a local case," Melanie said, "that led to the takedown of Todd Burk and a few Hellhound bikers. We were worried that Rip Lockwood and Ashley Russo had popped up on the Sandoval radar. Consequently, they had to go into hiding."

Monty knew them both. Ashley had worked for the sheriff's department. Her brother had been Holden's best friend in high school, before he was killed. They'd all suspected that Burk had been behind it. Monty had been thrilled when he'd learned of Burk's arrest. Justice finally served. "Yeah, I heard they picked up and disappeared. What does this have to do with me or the murder of Pandora Frye?"

"Welliver contacted me earlier," Melanie said. "Gave me the heads-up he was coming and why."

"Our inside man called me at two this morning. He's been trying to reach me for a couple of days, but he's being watched closely." Welliver sat on the edge of the desk, his expression grim, his eyes predatory, and Monty supposed one had to be a predator when hunting monsters. "Valentina Sandoval, the head of the cartel, has you in her crosshairs." He pointed at Montgomery.

"Me?" He stiffened. "Why?"

"After we talked a few hours ago," Melanie said, "I rushed into the office to see if I could figure out why. I cross-referenced your name with any cases related to the cartel. I got a hit on a big one." She offered the file and Monty took it. "Does the name Santiago Sandoval ring a bell?"

"Not really." He opened the folder. As soon as he saw the picture, it hit him. Dark eyes, slicked back hair, cocksure attitude. "I do remember him. He was speeding in a Mercedes-Benz G-Class. A two-hundred-thousand-dollar car. I expected a hard time. A smooth talker who wouldn't care about a hundred-dollar ticket. You know the type, it's more about the inconvenience. But this guy was different. A nasty piece of work. Real ballsy. He had a woman in the passenger seat, performing a sex act on him. She stopped at the last minute. He had white powder on his nose. There was more on the dash. When I questioned him about it, he offered me money. A lot of money. In cash. Boasted about how it was more than I make in a month. Told me to shut up, take it, get back in my vehicle and forget I ever saw him. Or there would be consequences. Life-and-death consequences."

"Of course you arrested the jerk," Waylon said.

"Of course." Monty nodded. "I did so with great pleasure, too. Turns out he had ten kilos of cocaine and one gram of fentanyl in the trunk. Along with a lot more cash."

"He was the son of Alejandro Sandoval," Melanie said. "Who used to run the cartel. Santiago was sentenced for possession with intent to distribute and received seven years in prison. His wife, who was in the passenger seat, got three years."

"Okay." Monty shrugged. "You do the crime, you do the time."

Welliver grimaced. "Not so simple. In prison there's a system, a code, a manner in which things are handled. Someone inside broke that code. A guard was probably paid off to move Santiago to a cell block where he didn't have protection. He died a very brutal, very violent death. It was slow. Painful. Real ugly. His father suffered a heart attack shortly thereafter, leaving Valentina in charge of the cartel and as guardian of her nephew, Santiago's son."

Ice ran through Monty's veins. "I take it she blames me. Because I didn't take the bribe and let him get away."

"Pretty much, yeah." Welliver sipped his coffee. "The reality is that she could blame Santiago's lawyer. The prosecutor on the case. The judge who sentenced her brother. The guard who was paid off. But you make an easy, simple source for her vehemence because probably in her twisted, dark mind it started with you. Makes it all your fault."

"Did your inside man give you anything else to go on?" Waylon asked. "Specifics?"

Welliver nodded. "Valentina asked him to assassinate your brother Holden. He made it look like he tried during the holiday tree lighting ceremony."

A hot blade of agony stabbed his chest. "She tried to have my brother murdered. But why?"

Welliver shrugged. "Because her brother is dead."

"But I've got a lot of brothers. Why would she single out Holden?"

"We've asked ourselves the same question. Best guess? He's the only one with a child," Melanie said. "I think that might be the reason, as disturbing as it sounds."

He swallowed down the raw bitterness rising in his throat.

"She also told my guy that she wanted him to do it in front of you, where you could watch. Valentina is a sadist. Next, she wants your father, Buck, to be executed. Her plan is to destroy everything you care about. Piece by piece."

Rage prickled his skin. "You think she's responsible for Pandora's murder."

Welliver tipped his head from side to side. "Stands to reason, considering I know she's behind Fiona Frye's death. She had my guy and one of her guards move the body and plant it in Amber Reyes's trunk."

Monty swore. "Why did she have to hurt so many other people? Why not just put a bullet in me and be done with it?"

"Too easy." Welliver smiled. "To her, you probably don't deserve a quick death since her brother didn't have one."

"But why kill Fiona?" Melanie asked. "To compound your guilt and implicate Amber?"

"I think there's more to it." Waylon moved to the edge of his seat. "Pandora was seeing a man. She had intercourse less than an hour before she died. My guess right there in her house, where you were blacked out. I think Pandora didn't fully trust this guy. Rightfully so. She gave her mother a flash drive with proof of who this man is and the nature of their relationship. Proof I'm sure we'll never find now."

"This guy is out there somewhere. In town." Monty stood. "My family isn't safe. None of them."

"I suggest you all go on lockdown at your ranch," the ADA said. "Lie low and wait it out."

"Wait? For how long?" Growing unease curled through his body. "Are you going to arrest Valentina?"

"For this?" Welliver asked.

"Yes!" Monty took a breath, doing his best to control his temper.

"Look, buddy, these are the facts." Welliver crossed his arms over his chest. "We have no proof that she's responsible for Pandora Frye's death. We have no proof that she ordered the murder of Fiona. Only that she had a body moved."

"What about my brother?" Monty asked in disbelief.

"Attempted murder for hire," Melanie said. "Solicitation carries the same potential penalty as the underlying crime. In this case, a conviction would carry a life sentence."

"There we go." He clapped his hands together once. "Make the arrest."

Welliver shook his head.

The ADA sighed. "This is her first offense. The judge will set bail. Probably somewhere between one hundred thousand and a quarter million."

"Chump change for her," Welliver said. "And what do you think she's going to do in the meantime? No need for suspense,

I'll tell you. Send the full force of her cartel to slaughter your entire family. And my guy will have been burned by then, so no more information from him. You won't see it coming. Not to mention she'll also put a hit out on my informant so he can't ever testify."

"What are you saying?" Monty asked. "There's nothing I can do?"

"We have to do more than arrest her," Agent Welliver said. "We need to cripple her business. Isolate her. And take down her crew as well."

"My family won't hide out at home indefinitely." Monty shook his head, sick with worry. "My mother is the mayor. My brothers are in law enforcement. They will feel obligated to do their jobs."

"Speaking of your mother," Waylon said. "I guess we should assume the embezzlement case that coincidentally popped up against her today is bogus."

"Based on the timing," the agent said, "in all likelihood."

"Listen, your ranch is a compound." The ADA met his gaze. "Call your family and have them muster there. Lock it down."

Monty nodded. He hated it, but she was right. "I need you to get my mother and Amber released from jail," he said to Waylon. "I'll call my father. He'll make sure they get to the ranch safely and he'll give everyone else a heads-up about what's going on."

"I'm on it. I'll call Chief Nelson. I can see if we can spare any officers to safeguard you guys at the ranch." Waylon took out his phone. "I also need to text Hannah about this."

"Don't ask for any police assistance," the DEA agent said. "We don't know who is in her pocket."

"You make a valid point." Waylon nodded. "Remember when I asked you about Officer Foley," he said to Monty.

"Yeah."

"He's the one who brought us the phone that was found

in your locker at work. He was also the one who pulled over Amber on a traffic stop and searched her trunk, where Fiona Frye had conveniently been dumped."

"I know him. I work with him," Monty said, exasperated. "He seemed like a good guy."

"They all do until they don't." The DEA agent strolled back to the window. "That's how it works in the underworld."

"The four of us need to put our heads together and map out how Valentina has done all of this," the ADA said. "She has more than Agent Welliver's inside guy helping her. Officer Foley is a possibility that we need to verify. He could be the tip of the iceberg. Until we figure out how deep this goes and who is involved, we don't know how much danger you or your family are truly in."

"You're right," Monty said. "Without knowing, my family and I are vulnerable, exposed, essentially operating blind." His gut burned.

If he didn't know the extent of the danger, how could he ever hope to keep his family safe?

Chapter Sixteen

Sunday, December 8
2:10 p.m.

To Amber, it was all a vicious blur. Seeing Fiona Frye in the trunk of her car. Being arrested. The mug shot. Having her fingerprints taken. Hauled to this awful cell and locked up.

She couldn't believe that having Holly in the cell next to her was comforting. Even though the accusation of embezzlement was unnerving. It seemed they were all being systematically targeted. But why and to what awful end?

"Honey, you can't keep stalling, sitting there simply holding your father's letter," Holly said.

Amber glanced down at the envelope in her hands. "I'm afraid."

"Of what?"

"I've been mad at him for so long, needing..." Her voice trailed off. She wasn't actually sure of what. "Something." An apology. An explanation that made her feel better. "And I'm scared that he won't give it to me in this letter. That I'll still be angry with him."

"Anger is the second stage of grief. As I see it, you've been grieving the loss of your relationship with him since you left. It's time to work through the other stages."

Amber shook her head. It couldn't possibly be that simple. Read a letter and work through the stages. Could it? "He should have told me that he was sick and given me a chance to fix this broken thing between us. Why would he deny me that closure?"

"Maybe it's in the letter. There's only way to find out." Holly leaned back against the wall. "My dad died on the job. Shot in the line of duty. He was healthy. In his prime. I never got to say goodbye to him either. But I would've given anything to have the kind of letter that you're holding now. It's a rare gift."

Amber swallowed hard. No matter how she felt after reading it, this was her father's final attempt at speaking to her. She owed him the respect of finding out what he had to say. She took a sip from her water bottle and opened the envelope.

Slowly, she removed the handcrafted white wove paper with the Longhorn Ranch logo embossed at the top and read the *handwritten* letter that she'd been carrying four months.

My Dearest Amber Sofia,
If you're reading this, then I have passed and, hopefully, I'm reunited with your mother. She was the love of my life. After hearing my last will and testament and the full terms of the trust, I'm sure you question that. Yes, I had an indiscretion many years ago. I have no excuse for it. Your mother was perfect, far too good for me, while I was a deeply flawed man who gave in to a stupid moment of weakness. The affair was short-lived because I realized that if Sofia ever found out it would break her heart. By that point, Fiona was pregnant and wanted to keep the child.

I provided for them, with the understanding that Sofia would never know the truth and Pandora would only learn I was her father when I was ready. Fiona agreed and waited for years. When your mother died, I was lost. Scared. Terrified about what would happen to you.

I didn't want you to be alone and I didn't want you to settle for less than you deserved.

You were my princess. I wanted to give you the world. I thought I could give you Monty. You loved him and I knew that he would love you in return one day. That he would make a strong, caring husband who would be a true partner through life. Also, through your union, our ranches could also be united. I never wanted to push either of you into ranching the way Buck did him. The boy only rebelled.

Buck treated him like he was a wild horse that needed to be broken. Tamed. But I saw something different. Monty is no horse. He's a mule. For one thing, they're smarter and can't be bullied. They need a legitimate reason to do what you want. "Because I said so" isn't good enough reason for them. You can't push them the way you can a horse and you have to have a ton more patience. Instead of using a whip, one must use love, understanding and a good reward system.

That's why I created the terms of the trust, as Machiavellian as it might have seemed. And it worked, too. Only weeks after you two became a couple, he was ready to marry you with a heart full of love, to be a faithful husband, a dedicated father to your children. But you found out about my machinations and split.

I can't say I blame you, my dearest. You have your mother's fire, her pride, her fighting spirit. I respect you for leaving and for turning your back on me.

My one regret is that I didn't apologize. It was the only way to get you to come back home. That or die. Ha ha! You see, I couldn't give you the apology you wanted, some heartfelt "sorry" because, well, I wasn't truly sorry. How could I be if I was willing to do it again?

And a million times over, I would do it.

You wanted Monty and I aimed to get him for you. Hence the reason I kept the trust as is. You never married. Monty never married. I must have faith in the belief that I have done the right thing and that you shall reap the reward even as I endured the price at not having you by my side in my final days.

Which brings me to Pandora. My child who suffered in my absence from her life, not having a father growing up though I lived in the very same town. She never had the memories and the birthdays, the celebrations, and the words of adoration from me. The hugs and kisses. My support or encouragement. To see the sparkle in my eye the way you did every time I looked at you. I can't ever give her those things. But I can give her the Reyes family home.

I know that one day you will call the Shooting Star Ranch your home. And Chance has moved on from Wyoming, and he doesn't care about the house.

Let Pandy have it with peace in your heart. Call her sister. Embrace her. Welcome her. If you don't, Chance never will.

Do this for me, though I have no right to ask anything of you. Please. I bet you can count on one hand how many times I've used that six-letter word with you and have fingers left over. Don't be angry with me anymore. Let it go.

Remember me. Toast me. Don't put flowers on my grave. Save those for your mother's. Pour a little whiskey on mine instead. The good stuff.

You are now and will forever be my sunshine.
Your Loving Father

Amber wiped the tears streaming down her face, but she couldn't stop crying. She was a total sobbing mess.

"Oh, honey, I wish I had some tissues for you," Holly said. "How was the letter?"

"You were right," she said, choked up. "A rare gift."

She suddenly missed her father so much and wished she could hug him. Hug him tight and tell him how much she loved him. That she was the one sorry and he was right about Monty. How he'd love to hear that. "You were right, Daddy," she whispered. "You were so right."

If only she had read the letter sooner. Before Pandora was murdered. She could've done as he requested. Maybe it would've made a difference somehow.

An officer came down the hall and stopped at their cells. "You're both free to go."

"Really, why?" Holly asked.

The cop shrugged and unlocked Amber's cell. "Orders from the chief."

Rubbing her swollen eyes, she rose to her feet and stretched her legs.

Next, he let Holly out. "Mr. Powell is waiting for you two."

Which Mr. Powell? Amber wanted to ask. There were so many of them.

Outside of the cells, Holly pulled her close, wrapping her in a warm hug. "You looked like you could use one of those."

She hugged her back, grateful for the affection. Having Holly and Buck as in-laws would be a mixed blessing. The best part was that they could tell her stories about her parents, things she didn't know, like the stuff about the bananas and lemon wedges. Stories that she'd be able to pass on to her own children even though her parents were gone. Their memories would live on.

"Thank you." Amber gave her a sad smile. "Let's get out of here and see who's waiting for us."

"My money is on my husband," Holly said.

Amber was relieved to leave the holding cell area and step into the hall on their way to freedom. "Even though we didn't get a chance to have the morning meeting you wanted, we still got to talk." It had been nice to have Holly there, for support, for comfort, for a friendly ear with no pressurizing discussion of the future and marriage.

"What meeting, honey?"

Amber furrowed her brow. "The one Vera called me about. She said you wanted to talk to me privately, away from the house."

"I didn't ask her to do that. There must be a misunderstanding. Maybe I made an offhand remark about wanting to speak with you and she took the initiative. She's helpful that way. Reading my mind, anticipating my needs."

"Must be nice to have such a helpful staff."

"I couldn't do this job as mayor without my team."

They passed the bullpen and could see the lobby. She spotted Buck and Eddie waiting for them.

As soon as they pushed through the double doors, Buck enveloped Holly in a bear hug and kissed the top of her head. She was a petite woman but looked even smaller and more fragile in her husband's arms.

"Why did they release us?" Holly asked. "Not that I'm complaining."

"Something to do with the Sandoval cartel and a woman named Valentina," Buck said. "Apparently, she's been targeting Monty. Wants to make him pay. All this misery we've been through over the past couple of days has been about a vendetta. She even tried to have Holden killed."

Holly gasped. "No."

Shock filled Amber's chest.

"That's what those shots fired at the tree lighting ceremony were all about," Buck said. "Goons from the cartel trying to take out our boy, Holden. I guess to punish Monty. We need to go to the Shooting Star. Arm up. Get the ranch hands in the bunkhouse to stand guard. And we'll wait for Monty. Once he has more information, we'll decide what to do."

"Where is Monty?" Amber asked. Why wasn't he here?

"He's working with Waylon, the assistant district attorney and a DEA agent. They're trying to figure out how deep this goes and who in town might be involved."

"Why is a DEA agent here?" Eddie asked. "Is it simply because it's about the cartel or are drugs a part of this?"

Buck shook his head. "I'm not entirely sure. Come on. We should get going."

"What about Grace?" Eddie pushed his glasses up his nose. "She and the baby are at the church. She was staying after service to help sort the donated toys for children in need. I hate to think about something horrible happening to her or poor little Kayce."

Holly pressed a hand to her chest. "Oh, no. Buck, we need to pick them up right away. I don't want her on the road alone. Unlike you and me she refuses to carry a gun."

"By the way," Buck said. "Here's your purse." He also handed Amber hers.

Holly took the handbag and checked the contents. "I need to buy her and you," she said, pointing to Amber, "a Beretta like the one I have. Small, but packs a deadly punch. Let's go to the church."

"Why don't you two go and get Grace and Kayce and I can take Amber to the ranch," Eddie said. "It's not best to have everyone clustered and so exposed. Two pregnant women and a baby all together? Makes for a tempting target. These cartel folks could have hired men lurking in every corner of the town."

"That's true." Holly put her purse under her arm. "But they're messing with the wrong family."

"Are you carrying?" Buck asked.

"Always." Eddie flashed the gun in his shoulder holster under his jacket.

"All right." Buck gave a firm nod. "You two go straight to the ranch. We'll be along shortly."

They hustled outside and separated, going toward different vehicles.

"Do you mind if we swing by my house first?" Amber asked. "I need to pick up some things. Clothes. My prenatal vitamins."

Eddie frowned. "Buck told us to go straight to the Shooting Star. We should listen to him."

"But there's no telling how long we'll be on that ranch." It wasn't like she could borrow stuff to wear from Holly or Grace. Neither would have anything that would fit her. Even Grace at almost nine months probably wore a size small in maternity clothing. "Please. I promise I'll be quick."

"Okay. Do you mind driving?" Eddie asked. "I've never been out to your place. That way instead of me focusing on directions, I can keep an eye out for anything suspicious. Worst-case scenario, if we were under attack, it would be hard to shoot at someone while driving."

"As long as it's not a stick. I'm not good with a manual."

"You've got nothing to worry about." He handed her his keys, and they climbed into his Chevy Tahoe.

Watching Buck and Holly speed in the direction of the church, she signaled and pulled out. At the corner, she turned onto Third Street and headed home.

Eddie was vigilant. Checking the rearview and side mirrors. Turning around and looking over his shoulder. Once they made it out of the busy part of town, he settled down.

It was easier to see someone trailing them or racing up behind the vehicle on Route 207.

"I have a small confession to make." A sheepish grin tugged at the corners of his mouth, and his brown eyes sparkled briefly.

"Please don't tell me you don't know how to fire a gun or aren't a very good shot," she said, half joking. She wouldn't have been surprised if that was the case, since he was such a gentle man with a quiet voice, disinterested in typical cowboy things like riding and shooting, but the odds were low. Most people raised in these parts or had lived here for a substantial amount of time learned to shoot and understood gun safety.

"Oh, no, it isn't that," he said. "I'm a rather good shot."

"Then what is it?"

"I wasn't entirely honest."

Longhorn River Road was coming up soon. "About what?"

"That you have nothing to worry about."

She glanced at him, trying to understand what he meant.

Eddie pulled his gun from the holster and aimed it at her.

Panic shuddered through her as her mouth fell open. "What are you doing?"

"Incentivizing you to do as I say. You're going to pass Longhorn River Road and make a left onto Big Canyon Way instead. Then we're taking Interstate 80 to I-25 South."

Her heart pounded, and her brain raced a million miles a second. "But why?"

"We need to go to Boulder."

She looked at him in shock, unable to keep her full focus on the road. "What's in Colorado? Why do we need to go there, Eddie?"

Taking a deep breath, he removed his glasses, setting them on the console between the seats. He peeled off his mustache, giving it a little yank that seemed to hurt. With a good, solid tug, he pulled the wig back, revealing a bald head. "Call me Roman. My boss is there," he said, his voice changing, deepening, hardening. His demeanor shifted, too, transforming before her eyes from unassuming into terrifying. "Valentina Sandoval. She's the head of the Sandoval cartel. One of the most powerful and ruthless individuals on the face of the planet." He spoke honestly without any affectation, and every muscle in her body vibrated with fear. "She's also the woman who wants to make Montgomery Powell suffer. Hence the need for you, the mother of his unborn child."

Chapter Seventeen

Sunday, December 8
2:50 p.m.

"Thank you. I appreciate the information." Monty hung up the phone. "My captain said that Nicholas Foley came in off patrol early on Friday afternoon. Claimed he wasn't feeling well. The camera showed him entering the locker room between shifts, when it wasn't busy and most likely empty, where he remained for less than five minutes and then left. But since we don't have cameras inside the locker room, we can't prove that he planted the phone."

"The flip phone had been wiped clean of any prints," Waylon said. "And there's no way it was coincidence that Foley was the same officer to pull over Amber. His story doesn't make sense. The guy lives way on the other side of town."

Monty grabbed one of the steaming hot coffees that had been brought in on a tray. "If Foley is a part of this, then his wife might be, too."

"Who's the wife?" the DEA agent asked.

"Vera. She's my mother's secretary in the mayor's office."

The ADA snapped her fingers. "Explains the neat packet of evidence that landed in Erica Egan's lap and made its way to the LPD. I'm sure that if we explain to her the extenuating circumstances, she might be willing to make an exception to her rule as a reporter and reveal her source for the story on your mother."

"I can light a fire under her," Waylon volunteered.

Monty gave a nod of gratitude. It was so much nicer to have this guy on his side rather than working against him.

There was a brief knock on the door before it opened. Hannah stalked in, shutting it behind her. "The bartender was lying. A guy came to see him on Friday morning after the murder. Broke into his house and woke up from a deep sleep. Terrified him. Paid him a thousand bucks to feed any cops that came sniffing around, asking questions, the story he told us and gave instructions to delete the footage. Threatened to kill him if he didn't."

"Did he give you a name?" Waylon asked.

"No, but he described the guy. Tan. Muscular. Not like a bodybuilder. But someone who works out. The guy could handle himself. Bald. Extremely scary. I showed him a picture of someone and it was the same guy."

"I don't understand," Monty said. "How do you have the guy's picture?"

"I was at Fiona Frye's house. It was ransacked. Someone was clearly looking for something and turned the place over good."

"He was looking for the flash drive." Waylon stood and stretched.

Monty happened to glance at the ADA and caught her watching the detective quite intently with unmistakable interest. Waylon's gaze flickered to Merritt's and a sly grin tugged at the corner of the detective's mouth a split second before the two looked away from each other.

The ADA and Waylon shared a mutual attraction, or they were discreetly involved. Either way, Monty saw the potential for problems.

"But he didn't find it," Hannah said with a smirk. She

pulled out an evidence bag from her pocket. Inside was a flash drive. "I did. Found it hidden in the bottom of a can of vegetable shortening in the pantry. Fiona was careful, too. When I popped the lid, it looked perfect. Brand-new. But something told me to dig."

"And our guy is on there," Waylon said.

"He is. Along with proof that the mystery man and Pandora were involved in a hot and heavy relationship."

"Let's see it." The ADA extended her palm. "We need to take a look at him."

"I can do you one better." She took out a folded-up paper from her jacket pocket and opened it. "I checked out the drive on one of the laptops Forensics had. Found a clear shot of his face and printed it." She slapped the eight-by-eleven-inch photo down. "It's him. That bald head is distinct, and Finn confirmed he was the one who paid him to lie and delete the security footage. The bartender was more afraid of this guy than of going to prison for obstruction of justice."

They all gathered around and peered at the picture.

Agent Welliver groaned. "That's Roman Cardoso. An enforcer turned lieutenant, holding the second highest position in the Sandoval cartel. He was Alejandro's right-hand man and is now Valentina's. If that man is in town," the DEA agent said, pointing to the picture, "then your family is in grave danger. I can't impress upon you how deadly this man is. He's not just a killer. He's clever. A seducer, snake charmer. A chameleon."

Chameleon. Monty stared at the picture. The eyes were familiar. Yet different. And there was something about the shape of the face that he recognized. "Give me a pencil."

Someone handed him one. He drew a pair of classic rectangular frames around the eyes, added a mustache and began filling in hair. A sledgehammer of horror slammed into Monty's chest.

"Dear God," Hannah said in a low voice, seeing exactly what he saw. "That's Eddie Porter. Your mother's assistant."

Eddie was always with his mother, attached at the hip. In the office. At the house. The man had unfettered access. "He's with my family right now." He whipped out his cell phone and hit the first speed dial—his father was number one, at the very top of his contacts. He was barely able to hear the numbers beep over the pounding of his heart in his ears.

"Thank goodness. I was about to call you," his dad said.

"Why? What's happened?"

"I—I—I don't even know how to say it. Monty..." His father's husky voice trailed off, only heightening his alarm.

His pulse quickened as he stared at the carpet. "Tell me what's wrong," he ordered, pressing his suddenly damp palm to his side. He'd never heard his dad, a man who was a stone pillar, unshakable, sound despondent. *"Tell me."*

"Amber's gone."

Monty drew in a sharp breath, his chest squeezing tightly. "What in the hell do you mean she's gone?"

"She left the police station with Eddie and they were supposed to go straight to the ranch, but they never made it here, Monty. I thought the cartel might've gotten to them on the road. But there's no sign of them of them anywhere. I've checked and her phone goes right to voice mail."

Rage churned in his stomach. "How could you let this happen?"

Silence. Sheer deafening silence over the phone.

"Son," his father croaked, with such despair echoing in the single word. "Monty... I'm so sorry."

Monty couldn't remember ever feeling this way, powerless, scared, spiraling out of control. But causing his father pain by blaming him wasn't going to solve anything. Eddie, that cunning viper, had fooled them all.

Focus. For Amber's sake, for the sake of our son. Focus!

He looked at the others in the room. "Eddie—Roman Cardoso—has Amber." He spoke through unbearable pressure swelling in his chest. "She's missing." The thought of her at the mercy of some sadistic kidnapper with a vendetta against him made his heart clench like a fist.

Agent Welliver let out a soft curse. "He's probably taking her to Colorado."

"You know where?" Monty asked.

"I don't know, son," his father said. "I'm so sorry."

"No, Dad. Not you. Hold on."

The DEA agent nodded. "Valentina has several places. My inside guy told me that Sandoval is in Boulder. I know the property."

Hope fired in his chest. "Then I'm going. With my brothers. We'll get her back."

Welliver shook his head. "You should let us at the DEA handle it."

No way was he waiting for approval and red tape to clear. "She might not have that kind of time. Boulder is a two-hour drive. We can arm up and strategize on the ride. Where is it?"

Welliver raked a hand through his thinning hair. "You and your brothers have no authority across state lines. I'll go with you. I can have some other agents meet us there. Trust me, you'll need every able body you can get. Valentina travels with an armed team. They are as capable as any paramilitary unit."

More manpower and more experience. He'd take it if didn't mean unnecessary delays. There wasn't a minute to spare. "No red tape?" Monty asked, wanting to be sure they were clear.

The corner of Welliver's mouth quirked up in a wicked grin. "I color outside the lines. A lot." His eyes flashed a predatory gleam. "I'll go hunting with you. No red tape."

Monty put the phone back to his ear. "Dad, tell my brothers we're going to get Amber. And ask Matt to bring his special toys." When Matt left the military, he took some Special Ops equipment with him. "It might come in handy since we're not entirely sure what we're going to be up against."

"We can cover you with almost anything you'll need, weapons, equipment," Welliver said. "We're used to this kind of thing. Trust me, we're prepared."

Monty gave a nod of thanks.

"I'll let the boys know," his dad said, "and I'm coming, too."

"Nope. You're not coming. You and Chance need to stay with Mom, Grace and the baby. Make sure you keep them safe."

"Chance won't like this anymore than I do," his father grumbled.

"He's the last Reyes male, the one expected to carry on his family name. If anything happened to him, I'd never forgive myself. Do what you can to make him see reason."

"Easy if I go with you and he does the babysitting."

"Mom would have a conniption. You're not going, Dad. You're needed at the ranch. That's final. Got to go." He hung up before his father could argue.

"Got room for one more?" Waylon asked.

Hannah clasped Monty's shoulder. "Make that two."

Monty nodded, the tightness in his chest easing a fraction at the show of support. "The more help the better."

4:35 p.m.

AMBER'S PULSE SKITTERED in her veins. She was in a warehouse filled with drugs and a small army of scary-looking men armed to the teeth. This was bad. Even if Monty was able to figure out where they were holding her, it would make a rescue problematic.

She stumbled into a small room on the second story, pushed by Roman. He shoved her down into a heavy metal chair bolted to the floor and restrained her to it using zip ties. Her gut knotted.

The fact he hadn't blindfolded her once during the trip and allowed her to see the abundance of drugs stored on the lower level didn't bode well at all.

"What do you hope to gain by this?" she asked him.

He sneered at her, and she ached to kick him between the legs, but she was bound and helpless.

"Gain isn't my goal," he said. "It's my pleasure and privilege to be of service. To Sandoval."

High heels click-clacked across the floor, close by, and an elegant woman appeared in the doorway. She wore varying shades of purple, from her silk top to her designer shoes. "You should understand, Ms. Reyes. Roman is talking about loyalty. To family. You're loyal, aren't you? To your brother. To the Powells. To Montgomery, no matter what he does."

"That's not true," she said, wanting to sound brave, but the tremble in her voice gave her away. "Monty hurt me once. I didn't stay with him. I didn't trust him, and I left. Because I deserved better."

"And now you think that's what he is. *Better*. Is that why you climbed back into bed with him? Had unprotected sex? Which requires a high degree of trust in my book. Why you're so excited to have to his child?"

Amber lowered her head. She didn't know how to answer. The truth would only confirm how much she loved him, putting her in more danger, and a lie would backfire since she wasn't good at pretenses. There was no winning if she played this woman's game.

"I get that you have a vendetta against him," Amber said. "That you want to hurt him. But why did you have to kill Pandora Frye?"

After reading her father's letter, she wished she'd had a chance to fulfill his wishes. To welcome and embrace the woman she had once unjustly hated.

"I didn't kill her." Valentina flashed a smile sweet as saccharine. "Roman did. As to why, well, her murder accomplished two objectives at once."

"First." She raised a single slender finger with a nail long as a talon. "Framing Monty for a crime that would land him behind bars for a considerable amount of time. And second..." Another finger lifted. "Gaining the power to destroy his family's legacy."

The land with the river. "But you lost that power when you killed Pandora."

Valentina quirked a brow. "Did I?"

"If I don't marry Monty—"

"Believe me, you won't live long enough to do that," Valentina said, cruelty radiating from every pore.

Amber drew a shuddering breath. She was scared. For her unborn child. She didn't want this precious life to be collateral damage in this woman's bloodthirsty quest for vengeance. "The land would've gone to Pandora," she continued, steeling her voice. "After you killed her, then it would've gone to her next of kin. Fiona. But for some sick, awful reason, you murdered her, too. Now the land will go to my brother." She thanked God that Chance was safe, far from the clutches of this vile woman. "He'll gladly give it to the Powells. So, you see, no matter what you do to me, the legacy of Monty's family will live on. It will thrive. It will grow. And there's nothing you can do about it."

Tapping a finger at the corner of her mouth, Valentina gave a mock frown. "Poor thing. You're two steps behind. Your little line of succession would be correct if Fiona had been Pandora's next of kin."

"I don't understand."

"Clearly. I'll spell it out for you." A Cheshire-cat grin spread over her face as she circled closer. "Fiona wasn't Pandora's next of kin. Roman is." She strutted up behind him and rubbed his shoulders.

"We were married last week," he said. "Our secret from everyone. Except *la jefa*."

This couldn't be happening. "You have a marriage license and had a ceremony?"

He nodded. "The whole shebang."

"A marriage to a fake person, to Eddie Porter, won't count." Monty and the rest of the Powells would piece it together.

He smiled, making him look even more terrifying somehow. "She married the real me. Roman Cardoso. A valid license. A legally binding marriage before her tragic and untimely death."

Amber reeled from the duplicity, the depths of evil. "But then why did you kill Fiona if she wasn't the next of kin?"

"She had evidence I was involved with Pandora. The mother might've been able to identify me."

"Why put her dead body in my trunk?"

"To wreak more havoc in Montgomery's life by framing you for murder and his mother for embezzlement. Next, I have wonderfully creative plans for the land," Valentina said, "none of which include the Powells ever getting their hands on it. Maybe I'll start with poisoning the river. Kill fifteen thousand head of cattle. That'll hurt. But I have so much more planned."

Dread burned up Amber's throat, lodging into a painful lump. "Please don't hurt me. Think of my unborn child. It's innocent in this."

"*He's* innocent," Valentina clarified. "Right? It's a boy. All the Powells are overjoyed."

This monstrous woman knew everything. Amber needed to think of a way out of this or she would be as good as dead. "You could just keep me hostage until January. Then it won't matter. I won't matter. The land will be Roman's."

Valentina tilted her head to the side and gave her a pitiable look that didn't reach her ice-cold eyes. "Aww, but you will matter. Montgomery Powell loves you. Hurting you will hurt him. That makes you a powerful bargaining chip. Whether you live or die will be up to him. I'm going to wait until you're dehydrated, hungry, writhing in pain. Then we're going to make a video. You're going to beg Montgomery to save your life. To save his son. All he has to do is kill an innocent person in public, in broad daylight, and turn himself in for the murder. Afterward you'll be released." Her tone was sincere but, in Amber's gut, she knew she was lying.

A slow, sick misery pooled in her stomach like raw sewage she wanted to expel.

This woman had no honor. And no heart. No matter what she did, Valentina Sandoval was not going to let her live. Fighting a jolt of panic, she took a deep breath. Becoming hysterical wasn't going to help. She had to stay strong.

When it came time for her to make the video, she wouldn't beg Monty to save her. She'd do the unexpected. She'd tell him to survive—that would be the sweetest victory.

If she was going to die, she'd do so without pleading. Fearless. On the outside, if not inside.

The only real chance she had of getting through this by some miracle was if Monty managed to find her before it was too late and came to the rescue.

She ached to wrap her arms around her belly, to protect her child. Shield him from any danger.

Hurry, Monty.

Please!

He had to save them both. It was her only chance.

Chapter Eighteen

Sunday, December 8
6:55 p.m.

Geared for battle, Monty and most of the team stormed the side of the hill overlooking the warehouse in Boulder, where they suspected Valentina Sandoval held Amber captive.

In total, they were ten, including Agent Welliver and three more guys from the DEA.

Two of Welliver's men and Waylon—the Bravo team—were covering the nearby residence, where Valentina was currently located. The inside man had eyes on her and had confirmed her presence as well as chatter about Amber being somewhere on the property. The warehouse looked like the most likely spot since the insider hadn't seen her or heard any mention of her being in the house. If the large building proved to be pay dirt for the DEA, with a cache of drugs, they'd arrest Valentina.

A massive seizure and the arrest of her crew would cripple her operation while she was behind bars. This was a golden opportunity to not only incarcerate her but neutralize her.

That woman had framed him for murder, gone after his brother, set up his mother, planned to kill his father and kidnapped the woman he loved, also endangering his unborn child. Monty needed to put an end to this to protect his entire family.

"Bravo team, this is Alpha. We're getting into position," Welliver said over the Bluetooth comms in their ears to the others waiting near the Sandoval residence, ready to take down Valentina.

Adjacent to the Eldorado Mountains, the grassy ridge was steep and the earth muddy, but they ate up the terrain in steady strides. He needed to clear his mind and focus his energy, but worry for Amber clouded everything.

Monty flattened against the tactical crest of the hill, below the actual peak where they had maximum visibility without advertising their position. Peering through the Eagle Eye scope, he swept the three stories of the warehouse. Cartel foot soldiers in tactical gear crawled throughout each floor. A fleet of black SUVs was parked outside.

"A freaking army down there," Logan said, lying in a prone position.

"We've got this." Matt's confident tone was to be expected.

He used to be Special Forces for years before he had enough of the bloodshed and came back home. This sort of thing had been routine for him.

The only other person with combat experience, DEA aside, was Waylon, but Monty had no idea what the scope and breadth of his skills were, only that he appeared just as at ease as Matt before they had separated.

Holden nudged Agent Welliver. "The size of that crew down there is a little intimidating. We're outnumbered and out-manned. Any chance of getting us some additional backup?"

The seasoned DEA agent chuckled, the sound sharp-edged and almost homicidal. "Nope. Afraid not. This is the best I could do on short notice with no red tape."

Popping cinnamon gum in his mouth, Matt said, "I only see guns and knives down there. We have a force multiplier." He indicated the grenades the DEA had passed out.

They had three varieties, the primary being smoke. Flash

and stun were the other two. The former would act as a great distraction, issuing three to seven loud reports—explosions— each accompanied with a flash. The latter had a more devastating effect. A stun grenade had one huge explosion of up to 185 decibels and an eleven million candlepower flash. Used in a small room it would rupture eardrums and cause temporary blindness.

In a warehouse environment, a stun grenade could buy them anywhere from eight to twelve seconds. Not much time but enough to disarm and incapacitate a gunman if they didn't hesitate.

Welliver had also provided them with top-of-the-line comms, bulletproof vests, helmets and other equipment they needed to help locate Amber. He gave the signal to a younger agent, Jasper Pearse, who deployed the drone fitted with a thermal camera. They were particularly useful for finding a missing person because of their ability to detect heat and temperature differences.

The drone circled the building going one floor at a time from top to bottom until Pearse isolated her probable location. "Look here." Pearse pointed out clusters of men in various sections. Then he brought the drone back around to the second floor, over to a back corner. A solitary heat signature was seated in a small room. "I think that's her."

"Our best bet," Monty said, agreeing with the assessment.

"Let's get this party started." Welliver slung the strap of a grenade launcher over his shoulder. "Once we get close to the building, we should split up. Some go high and some go low. Sweep the building from the bottom up and top down in tandem."

"High," Matt said.

"I'll go with him," Logan volunteered.

Monty flicked off the safety on his personal 9mm, and they swept down the hill in a V-formation with Welliver leading the way. Anxious energy wired him tight.

Off on Monty's left flank, Matt and Logan took out the gunmen on the east side of the building in a controlled sweep of muzzle-suppressed fire.

Once they came within spitting distance, Welliver held up a fist, bringing them to a halt. The team flattened up against the east side of the building while Pearse whipped out two grenades of white phosphorous. Slipping on gas masks, they prepped to breach the building and pop smoke.

Matt and Logan needed time to cut around to the north side of the building to a fire escape before the rest of them entered the building.

Pearse was tracking a countdown on his watch. He gave a vigorous nod once it was time, pulled the pins on two grenades from his pack, yanked open the door and pitched them inside.

A barrage of bullets sprayed the steel door. In ten seconds, thick white smoke would conceal their ingress and throw the Sandoval soldiers off balance.

Pearse gave the go-signal with another sharp nod and opened the door. They rushed inside, peeling off in different directions.

Dense smoke wafted throughout the entry of the industrial space, not quite reaching the high ceiling where metal ductwork ran in heavy rows. On the first level old machinery served as excellent cover for the enemy. Dark figures darted in between concrete pillars and rectangular objects—cases or boxes—digging in for the fight.

The Alpha team fanned out and moved in. Monty was keeping a close watch-out for hostiles in any sniper positions as he maneuvered across the wide warehouse floor. But there was no telling how many of the cartel's foot soldiers lurked. He eased to the far wall, looking for a different angle to exploit.

Wearing a bulletproof vest and sleek tactical helmet, he followed the path of huge ductwork along the ceiling to a wall and series of pipes.

Gunfire came from the far side of the space. Controlled bursts from armed men sweeping in toward the entrance where he'd last spotted Hannah and Holden. They were no doubt picking off targets.

With the chaos and noise of the gunfire, they were operating with limited communication. The one equalizer: the cartel soldiers were functioning under the same conditions.

Monty skirted the wall, scanning for hostile movement, until he hit a barrier. A half wall, maybe an office or, from the heavy industrial look of the space, an old clean-air room used to house special AC equipment.

Testing the stability of a pipe connected to the wall, he shook it. Solid. Risking exposure by climbing up was necessary to find an avenue to gain the upper hand. He holstered his gun and scrabbled up, using the bolted brackets for footholds and handles. Sweat dripped from his forehead under the gas mask, rolled down his temples and pooled under his chin.

His hands found a three-foot-wide gap between the pipe and office-type structure. He pushed off the pipe, gripping onto the top of the self-contained space. Hoisting himself onto the roof, he didn't make a sound. Ten feet of clearance to the ceiling and high above the layer of phosphorous.

Crouching, he stayed low and removed his mask. The smoky air below was dense and heavy in pockets where the grenades had gone off. He scanned the area. Open crates of drugs packaged for possible shipment were lined up in rows.

They had confirmation of drugs. "We've got thousands of kilos in here," he said to Welliver.

Six dark-clad figures circled closer to Hannah and his brother Holden.

An electric energy pumped hot through him. He locked sights on the two closest to them. A couple of soft squeezes on the trigger, and the men dropped. More stun grenades were used. Systematically, they either eliminated or incapacitated the rest of the cartel men on the first floor. Waylon was making his way to a staircase and signaled for them all to advance while Pearse covered the rear.

Confident no more hostiles remained on this floor, Monty jumped from the office structure, landing on the balls of his feet. Pain torpedoed his knees, but he blinked it away, hustling to join the others at the stairs.

They tried to take a furtive peek to see what waited for them on the next floor.

A wave of bullets rang out in a striking clang. Suppressive fire swept over the metal staircase to keep them from ascending.

Backs against the wall, Welliver pointed to his own eyes, then the stairwell. Pulling out a telescoping-wand camera that allowed tactical viewing without getting your head blown off, he ventured to the edge of the staircase to determine the location of the gunmen.

Welliver shifted the wand around the corner for a complete picture. He slipped back beside Monty. "Two shooters. One at the top of the stairs. The second is leaning over the railing. They're taking turns with bursts of fire."

It would require someone to drop to the ground on their back to take the shot. Someone precise. Decisive. Sharp.

"From what you told me," Welliver said to Monty, "you might be better suited for this. Young back and all." He grinned.

On the ride to Boulder, Monty had told him about the marksmanship training he'd had growing up. He loved ranching and shooting. The more his father had hounded him about legacy, the more Monty had focused on handgun and long-range rifle shooting. As a state police officer, he'd aced marksman sniper training.

No doubt the older agent had a ton of field experience, but Monty was probably a better shot.

Now that they knew the setup of the shooters, he listened.

For the pattern and rate of fire. The one at the top, leaning over with a sweeping view of the steps, was the most dangerous and needed to be eliminated first.

Waiting for his blink-of-an-eye window to open, Monty removed his tactical helmet. Not a reckless choice. A calculated one. He couldn't chance the gear getting in his way, throwing him off a centimeter.

The bottom stairs cleared of gunfire for a breath, the shooters prepping to reload. Monty dove, sensing where to aim as much as sighting the targets. He fired, rolled, readjusted and squeezed the trigger again. The first man hit the staircase with a bullet to the head. The second took a slug to the chest.

Monty climbed to his feet. "Did you see all the drugs they've got in crates?" he asked Welliver.

"Yeah. Better than what we could've expected."

"Give the order. Before someone tells Valentina that we're here and she gets away." He couldn't let that happen. "Do it now. There's no reason to wait."

"Bravo team," Welliver said over comms, "you're cleared hot to take the queen. We've got powder. Lots of powder."

"Roger that," another agent responded. "We're going in."

Monty hoped Waylon and the other agents apprehended Valentina Sandoval fast.

Turning his focus back to finding Amber, he bounded up the steps. Quick. Quiet. The others were right behind him.

The landing opened onto the second floor. No corners, no walls to hide behind immediately. That meant exposure at the top of the stairs. Whatever was waiting could hit them full force.

Bracing against the railing, Monty slipped his helmet on. "Be ready to use flash grenades," he said to the rest of the team. "I don't want Amber getting hurt if we use something more aggressive or her getting caught in the middle of a shoot-out."

Welliver held up a stun grenade. "Bigger impact. It would be better."

"You're probably right," Monty said, understanding the disadvantage it would put them at, "but Amber is pregnant. Flash only around her. I won't take the risk. Got it?"

Everyone nodded.

Pounding footsteps resounded on the first floor, drawing closer. Someone must've called for reinforcements to circle around behind them.

"We'll go hold them off," Hannah said, referring to herself and Holden.

Pearse tapped her on the shoulder. "I'm with you guys."

The three of them took off back down the stairs.

Poised near the top of the landing, Monty was ready to bolt up and try to get to cover. He glanced back at the senior agent.

"I'll cover you from here," Welliver said. "And make sure no one gets past those three downstairs and sneaks up on your rear." The agent took a defensive posture on the stairs, the only position affording cover.

Glass shattered on the floor above them. A flurry of activity up there followed. Guns were chambered followed by a riot of gunfire. Logan and Matt must've breached the third floor.

Now or never. Monty raced up the last few steps, rushing onto the second-floor landing. Quickly, he got a look, spotting Amber, and ducked to the left, taking cover behind a wall.

The man he had known as Eddie Porter, kind and agreeable and soft-spoken, was gone. In his place was the cruel-looking Roman Cardoso, holding a gun pointed at Amber's head, using her as a shield.

Relief trickled through him. She was alive. Possibly fatigued and dehydrated, but otherwise she didn't appear hurt.

If this got to the point of some feigned negotiation, Monty realized he could lose the woman he loved along with his unborn child. He needed to act first and seize the advantage.

"Come on out, with your hands up!" Roman said. "Or I'll shoot her!"

Monty steeled himself for what he had to do next. He grabbed two flash grenades. Pulled the pins with his teeth. Released the spoons. Counted to two and tossed them into the wide-open space littered with ratty furniture and large crates.

The grenades clanged to the floor. Rolled and detonated.

With the first two pops, he drew his weapon and stormed inside. Roman had released her and was trying to get to cover. Amber had her hands over her ears, with her eyes shut as she crouched beside a stone pillar.

Monty hustled inside and grabbed her by the arm. Shuffling backward, keeping his eyes trained on the room, he ushered her toward the stairs.

Welliver lunged forward, taking hold of her arm. He got her down out of the line of any possible incoming fire.

This wasn't over. No way was he going to leave Roman Cardoso in there to come after his family.

Monty swooped back into the room. He slipped up behind a pillar and then dashed to the next. A figure ran behind one of the crates near the sofa. *Gotcha!* Monty stalked closer to the crate, his weapon up and at the ready.

A man leaped up, holding an AR-15 rifle, and Monty fired, hitting him square in the chest. Just a nameless soldier. As the guy dropped to the floor, another man—packed with lean muscle—lunged, tackling Monty and knocking his gun loose.

Monty let the momentum carry him, flowing into the fall. He drove his knees into Roman's torso, flipping him overhead. Moving fast, Monty spun and sprang upright, sending a blow to the man's forearm, dislodging the weapon. But Roman followed up, throwing a punch toward him. Monty twisted sideways. The fist barely missed his face and rammed into his shoulder, knocking him into a forty-five-degree spin.

Staggering backward, Monty struggled to right himself.

Roman bent down, reaching for something on his ankle. Another gun appeared in his hand.

Adrenaline flaring through him, Monty didn't hesitate. He threw a sideways kick into Roman's wrist. The pistol discharged before it flew from his hand, skittering out of reach.

The slug slammed into the concrete pillar beside Monty. Close. Too close. Another inch or two and the bullet would've hit his abdomen. Not slowing for a beat, Monty kept moving. But Roman was ready for him. Vicious kicks and punches were exchanged back and forth. But Monty couldn't afford to lose, couldn't give this man the slightest advantage.

A brutal punch struck Monty's cheek, another in his ribs, pounding the air from his lungs. The taste of metallic salt hit his tongue.

Monty butted his skull into Roman's head and jabbed a fist into his exposed throat, bringing the guy to his knees. *I've got him!* Now he needed to end this.

A flash of metal glinted.

By the time Monty registered the knife, it was too late. Roman stabbed the large blade into his thigh and twisted it. White-hot agony tore a scream from his lips.

Roman lowered his shoulder and slammed it up into Monty's chest with the force of a battering ram, taking them both to the floor.

A desperate, violent need to shut this man down eclipsed everything else. Monty sent his elbow crashing into the head of the dangerous man who had infiltrated his home and threatened his family. He knocked Roman to the side, but the guy scrambled quicker than lightning. Roman made it up, spotted something on the floor—a gun—and grabbed the pistol.

Breathless and face bleeding, Roman aimed the 9mm at Monty's chest.

His blood chilled at the split-second thought of failing Amber. Of losing her and his baby. Blinking it away, he vaulted at the guy, unarmed, screaming through the gut-wrenching pain in his leg, determined to protect his family. Even if he had to die to do it.

A distinct pop punctured the air, and a shudder ripped through Monty.

The hot slug made Roman's head jerk back on impact. He staggered a step and dropped to his knees and keeled over, dead.

Monty glanced over his shoulder.

Logan stood holding a gun.

The stark fear gripping Monty in a fist-tight hold dissolved as a rush of peace filled him. "I've never been happier to see you."

Logan grinned. "I've got your back. Always."

Yeah, his little brother did. Lucky thing, too, otherwise he'd be the one dead on the floor.

Logan glanced down at Monty's leg, noticing the injury. He hurried to his side.

Monty slung his arm over his brother's shoulder. Matt met them at the landing of the stairs and came up on the other side of him. The two supported Monty, helping him hop down the stairs.

"The queen is dead," Waylon said over comms. "She opened fire. We had to take her out. All of Bravo is fine."

It was over. The nightmare was finally finished. Roman and Valentina were dead. The threats to his family had been eliminated.

His brothers helped Monty limp through the warehouse and outside into the fresh air. Hannah, Pearse and Holden were right behind them. They made their way back to the other side of the hill.

Welliver had gotten Amber to safety and secured inside one of the vehicles they had driven. She spotted him and bolted from the SUV.

He didn't want her to run, but also couldn't wait to hold her in his arms.

She rushed to him, wrapping him in a tight hug, her trembling body crushed to his, and nothing in the world had ever felt better.

Amber pulled back and stared at his leg. "Oh my God. Are you all right?"

"I think I will be." It hurt like hell, but he had Amber, he was on his feet, breathing, and they hadn't sustained any casualties. He couldn't complain.

"We've got to remove it," she said.

"No," several voices said in unison.

He met her frantic gaze. "I could bleed out," he said, with a sad smile. "Best to let a doctor do it."

She threw herself into his arms again, and he basked in the warmth of her embrace, the surety of her touch. No more skepticism. No more hesitation. No more fear.

Raw emotion flooded him, replacing the adrenaline high. He bent down to look into her eyes and smiled at the love shining on her face.

"We need to get him in the vehicle," she said to his brothers.

They helped him hobble over and got him inside. She found a medical kit and climbed in on the other side. The others hung back, giving them a moment alone together.

"Are you all right?" he asked, looking her over.

She nodded as she took gauze out of the kit. "Once I get your leg wrapped to slow the bleeding, I'll grab a bottle of water." She bandaged his thigh as best she could around the Bowie knife lodged in it.

The pain was intense. He'd never felt such agony.

But Amber was all right. His son was all right.

He pressed a palm to her cheek. "I'm so thankful you're not hurt. I imagined horrible things. What they could've been doing to you. I couldn't bear the thought of losing you. Either of you."

She placed her index finger against his lips. "No more imagining the worst. No more regrets. No more looking backward. From this day forward, we're together. A family. No matter what. I love you, Montgomery Beaumont Powell, and I want to marry you as soon as possible."

The words curled around his heart like a warm embrace. He cupped her jaw and gave her a soft kiss. "Are you sure?"

"I'm one hundred percent positive about everything. That I want to marry you. That you truly love me, with or without the land."

"You just went through something horrendous. You might not be thinking straight. We can wait. Stick to the plan. I don't mind."

"We can't stick to that plan because I do mind. It's selfish and rooted in fears that I no longer have." She took his free hand and put it on her rounded belly. "Our son, your brother's children, Kayce and the baby coming in weeks, and all the other little ones on the way deserve their birthright. The Powell and Reyes legacy. We need to protect it, fight for it, not take it away from them."

Joy ballooned in his chest until he could barely breathe. He was in so much pain but had never been happier. "How did I get so lucky to have you?"

"Fate." She shrugged. "Or a wise father's keen insight and persistent machinations."

Smiling, he pulled Amber into his arms and then gave her a heart-pounding kiss that rocked him to his core. "Whether it was fate or your father or both, I know that we were always meant to be together. Joined as one."

Epilogue

Three months later
5:50 p.m.

"What do you think about Beaumont, my grandfather's name?" Monty asked, his voice rough and husky, making her bare skin tingle.

She turned over onto her back, lying in their bed in the cottage that had been built for them a decade ago, and stared at him. "Beau," she whispered, a soft smile surfacing on her face, and nodded. "Could we name him Beaumont Carlos?"

He kissed her on the lips. "Has a great ring to it, but it could be whatever you want. We could name him Peanut if it makes you happy. Peanut Powell has a ring to it also." Then he kissed her full belly and the baby kicked hard. "Oh, I felt that one. A good pop to my mouth. I guess baby says no to being officially named Peanut."

They laughed.

Fully naked, he rolled out of bed and crossed the room, grabbing his boxer briefs from the chair. He still had a slight limp from the knife wound in his thigh and the doctors told him he always would. That made him unfit to continue with the state police, but when he heard the news, a weight lifted from him, and he acted at peace with giving up the badge.

Now he was a full-time rancher in charge of the Shooting

Star-Longhorn. His choice. He woke early with a sense of purpose and pride. He went to bed after loving her and cuddling, a happy kind of tired from the work, without a care in the world. Slept blissfully, soundly, with his arm draped over her.

Things on the ranch were delightfully dull. No danger. No dead bodies. After the reporter Erica Egan gave up Vera Foley as her source on the embezzlement case against Holly, Waylon had managed to squeeze a confession out of her. She admitted to forgery, being the one to embezzle money from the city, and working for the Sandoval cartel along with her husband Nicholas.

"There's something I never asked you," she said.

"Fire away."

"Why did you move into this, our house, after I left?"

"Two reasons. One, it was penitence. To be reminded every day, every second I was here of what I did wrong. Two, I was waiting for you."

She smiled. "Did you ever bring anyone here? A woman? You can tell me. I won't be mad."

"Bring another woman to our house? No, sweetheart, I never did that." Monty slipped the boxers on up to his trim waist.

Nibbling her lower lip, she couldn't tear her gaze from his marvelous body, strong legs, sculpted arms, washboard abs, a dusting of hair on his muscular chest. A spectacular specimen of a man. With his tawny hair a beautiful mess from their lovemaking and the evening stubble on his jaw, he looked rugged. Sexy. Perfect.

Squeezing her thighs together, she ached deep in her core to have him again. She glanced down at the diamond wedding band on her finger. Every time she looked at it her heart danced in her chest. *I'm Mrs. Montgomery Powell.*

An uncontrollable rush of pure joy suffused every cell in her body.

"What are you thinking right this second?" he asked, the expression in his eyes dark and alluring.

She loved the way he looked at her. Like she was the most beautiful, precious creature that he'd ever seen.

"About you. How happy I am to be your wife and that we got married on New Year's Eve."

It had been a gorgeous, candlelit evening ceremony at the ranch with the entire family and a few old friends from town. Some new ones too, such as Waylon. It had been small and intimate. She wore an empire-waist dress, her hair full of curls pinned high. He wore a tailored navy suit. They dined on filet mignon and sea bass and had three different flavors of wedding cake. Vanilla with passionfruit curd, a layer of purple huckleberry, and lemon with raspberry filling. Everyone danced until the stroke of midnight when fireworks burst into the sky, ringing in the New Year and celebrating their nuptials.

The only thing missing was her mother helping her get ready and her father walking her down the aisle, but Holly and Chance were pleased to fill in.

She missed her parents and her dad's meddling, but she'd worked through the stages of grief and was finally at the stage of acceptance.

Her life was full and rich and overflowing. She was grateful to be surrounded by so much love and support. To have such a large family where she got to see her nieces and nephews grow up. To be close to them. To have huge dinners where they all gathered, their lives inextricably intertwined. To call this ranch her home as her father always knew she would. Where their son would be raised.

Monty came back to the bed, leaned in, cupped her breast and gave her a deep, hot kiss. She pulled back and looked at him. Heat flickered in his eyes.

Laughing, she tapped his nose. "Don't even think about it,

mister. Holden will be dropping the kids off for us to baby-sit any minute."

Grace had given birth to the most beautiful little girl, Nova. Six pounds, seven ounces. The baby came two weeks early and she was only in labor for three hours. Another easy baby with a sweet temperament.

"You know, we could always get Mom and Dad to watch them." His timber-rough voice sent a shiver along her spine. He cupped her breast again and ran his thumb over her pert nipple.

Hot waves of awareness coursed between them.

"Don't you want to practice being parents, Monty? We're going to have our own soon."

"Oh, I want to practice all right. Practice making babies. This one might be a fluke."

Her smile fell as she realized they still hadn't discussed something.

"What's wrong, sweetheart?" He rubbed her arm. "Was it something I said? I don't want you to feel like I'm always all over you and you can't get a break. It's just you're so sexy." He beamed at her, sending a flutter through her chest.

"No, it's not that." Looking at the bed, she took his hand. "How would you feel if this baby was a fluke?"

"What do you mean?"

"The doctors told me it would be difficult for me to get pregnant. Next to impossible. Because I have a blocked fallopian tube as a result of surgery I had for endometriosis. What I'm saying is that this little guy is our miracle baby." She lifted her eyes to his. "He might be our only baby. I don't know if I'll be able to give you more children. I'm sorry. You wanted a big family. We should've talked about it before we got married instead of rushing."

He crushed his mouth to hers in a toe-curling, stomach-dropping kiss. "We already have a big family. Proof will be knocking at our door dropping off two babies in a minute. If our son is an only child, I guarantee he'll never be lonely. Not with his cousins living on the ranch." He smiled at her. "No imagining the worst. No regrets. It's you and me and this little one." He rubbed her belly. "No matter what. Right?"

A burst of all-consuming happiness rushed over her.

Monty stroked her cheek so tenderly that tears sprang to her eyes. "Don't be sad, sweetheart. This house is going to be full of kids we love. Trust me."

"I'm not sad. These are happy tears. I promise." She sat up and leaned against his chest.

Wrapping his arms around her, he hugged her tight, and she sank into the embrace, certain he would never let her go.

"Come on," he said. "We've got a reputation to earn. The best uncle and aunt ever. I want that top-dog status of *favorite*. Let's get dressed. We've got to entertain two kids under two until they run us ragged to the bone."

She laughed. "I can't think of anything else I'd rather do."

"Well, I've got a couple of ideas." He winked at her.

* * * * *

Read on for a preview of the next book in the Cowboy State Lawmen: Duty and Honor series by Juno Rushdan.

Chapter One

It was another typical Thursday evening until it wasn't. A fourteen-hour workday. Always the first one in. Always the last one out.

Gathering her things, she grabbed the fragrant bundle of flowers from a chair and then closed the door to her office. She glanced at the plaque on the door, engraved *Assistant District Attorney, Melanie Indira Merritt*.

"One day it won't be *assistant*," she muttered to herself. Her time would come.

Melanie had put in tremendous effort and had the keenest talent when it came to picking a jury, leading to her pristine victory record, and earning her the nickname of The Closer.

Her previous boss had a bad habit of taking credit for her work, but things were different at her position here in Laramie, Wyoming. This DA didn't use her and didn't try to sleep with her. More of a father figure, Gordon championed her successes, invited her into his home for meals with his wife and helped make her transition to the Cowboy State a smooth one.

She walked down the hall of the third floor of the county courthouse, where the prosecuting attorney's offices took up the entire space, and locked the inner door. Her stomach grumbled, reminding her she'd missed dinner.

Adjusting the straps of her laptop case and purse on her

shoulder, she glanced at her watch: 9:10 p.m. Too late for anything heavy. A Caesar salad waited for her in the fridge.

She pushed through the outer door into the attached covered parking garage. The muggy July wind had died down and cooled off. A light rain had started. In the Wyoming valley, where Laramie and Bison Ridge sat, surrounded by the mountains, the temperature in the summer evenings was often mild and pleasant, which beat a blustery winter breeze slicing through her.

She watched Darcy Rosenfeld pull out of her parking spot. The paralegal was great at helping her prepare for meetings and trials. The young woman was thorough, saving Melanie tons of time.

At the trash receptacle, Melanie stopped and took one last whiff of the bouquet of flowers cradled in her arm. Roses, freesia, sweet pea, peonies and hyacinth. Her favorites. They smelled divine, rich in summer colors that would brighten anyone's day.

She read the card once more.

To M&M-no nuts,
This sucks. I hate it. I miss you. Miss the us that might've been. Please rethink this. Soon. Can't wait forever.
Your Cowboy

Melanie bit back a sad smile. Waylon was holding on to false hope that she would backtrack, go against common sense and a healthy instinct for professional self-preservation. At least he'd stopped calling and leaving enticing voicemail messages that tested her willpower.

He needed to move on. They both did, but she was far too busy to find someone more suitable, who wasn't a threat to her career.

She tossed the gorgeous bouquet into the trash bin.

Darcy pulled up and rolled down her passenger's side window. "I'd kill for Hank to buy me a bouquet like that," she said, referring to her boyfriend, a sweet paralegal at a local firm. "Maybe I'll drop a hint. Hey, even if the relationship is kaput, you should keep the flowers. Must've cost a fortune. Sure you don't want to tell me who the cowboy is? It'll be our secret."

Sharing was how secrets ceased to exist. "Good night, Darcy. See you tomorrow." She waved bye.

"Your cowboy, whoever he is, has excellent taste. Not only in flowers." The grinning paralegal drove off.

Part of Melanie ached for Waylon. He was unlike any man she'd been with. A salt-of-the-earth straight shooter. Humble. Handsome despite his scars or perhaps because of them. Emotionally available.

A great lover.

And a crackerjack detective with the Laramie Police Department, constantly arresting dangerous criminals she had to prosecute.

Therein lay the complicated problem.

When it came to choosing the right guy, she was a horrible failure.

Loneliness crowded in on her. She reached into the trash bin and took out the flowers, against her better judgment. They'd die in a week on their own. No need for her to hurry their demise. Besides, Darcy was right. Waylon had paid a pretty penny for the huge bouquet. She'd never chuck a hundred-dollar bill out the window because the wrong person had given it to her.

A yawn took hold. She needed to get home, eat and rest. So she could rise and shine at the crack of dawn, go for a run and do it all over again.

Yay, me.

Pulling her car keys from her purse, Melanie headed for her SUV, the lone vehicle remaining on the top level, tucked beside a concrete pillar. Her keys jangled in her hand and her high heels click-clacked across the pavement, echoing in the garage. Raindrops pitter-pattered on the roof of the building and asphalt on the street. She liked to park midway in the lot. Far enough to get in some extra steps on her pedometer. But not too far to make her uncomfortable at night in the public parking garage alone.

These past six months without Waylon, she was always alone.

Maybe it was time for her to get a pet. A fluffy, warm independent cat to cuddle. Too bad she was allergic.

She pressed the button on her fob—the horn beeped, and the lights flashed—unlocking the SUV—and dropped the keys into her suit pocket.

Footsteps shuffled somewhere behind her. The nape of her neck prickled as she wheeled around toward the sound.

No one. Not a soul in sight.

She listened.

Silence, other than the rain.

She scanned the nearly empty upper floor, searching for anyone lurking, any sinister shadows in dark corners, but she didn't see anything of concern. Nothing out of the ordinary.

Was her mind playing tricks on her? Served her right for working herself to the bone every day.

Dismissing it as fatigue, she started for her truck. She walked with care, trying to lessen the clatter of her heels.

More footsteps—the sound whispering beneath the noise of her shoes.

Unease slid down her spine. She stopped and surveyed her surroundings again with even more vigilance.

This was a small town, where everyone knew everyone. None of the dangers of a big city, like random muggings, drug addicts driven to desperation. Crime still existed. Usually of a higher order.

Looking around, she didn't see anyone.

The lot was well lit, the street below quiet. The sheriff's office was in the same building on the first floor, and she was well acquainted with everyone in the department. An attendant was in the booth on the main level until ten o'clock. She was fine.

Perfectly safe.

Still…

Tension gnawed at the base of her spine.

Trust your instincts. That was what her parents and self-defense classes had taught her.

She tightened her grip on the leather straps of her bags. Digging in her purse for her cell phone just in case, she hurried her pace to her car. Her pulse picked up. Sweat trickled in a cold line down her back. Almost there.

Almost.

Movement out of the corner of her eye snatched her attention. She whirled back around.

A man lunged from behind a concrete pillar and rushed toward her. Dressed in dark clothing. Wearing a full-face helmet. Dark tinted visor. Something long and metallic in his hand.

A crowbar!

Her heart seized. She stumbled backward.

He plowed into her, shoving her up against her vehicle. The flowers tumbled from her arm. He raised the steel bar and swung. She ducked, narrowly missing the blow intended for her skull that crashed against the car roof instead.

Melanie punched his stomach and rammed her knee up into his groin. With a grunt, he doubled over and staggered away. She jerked sideways and ran. But he snatched the back of her suit jacket, stopping her.

"Help! Help me!"

Grabbing the laptop case's strap, she swung the bag, using it as an improvised weapon. She slammed it down against his arm, freeing herself of his grip. But her purse slipped off and fell. Another swing with all her strength knocked the crowbar from his other hand and it clattered to the concrete floor. She kicked the steel bar, sending it skittering under the car. Then she slung the laptop case up at his head.

He lurched back, his arms flailing.

She dropped the bag and took off running, cursing her stupid heels and the tightness of her skirt. Taking the ramp would lead to the attendant booth and the sheriff's office. But her assailant was faster and stronger. He could easily overtake her on the way down two stories. Same problem with the stairs.

Keys jangled in her pocket. Avoiding both the ramp and staircase, she bolted back toward the building.

Footsteps thundered after her. Melanie flung the exterior door open and ducked inside. She dared to look back. Through the glass panel, she spotted him. He was up and running straight for her.

She raced for the interior door to the office space and snatched the keys from her pocket.

Faster, faster! Run faster!

The keys slipped from her fingers, hitting the carpet. She dashed back and grabbed them. With shaking hands, she fumbled for the right one.

Hinges squeaked behind her. She cast a terrified glance over her shoulder. He stormed through the outer door leading from the garage. She shoved the key into the dead bolt and unlocked the frameless glass door.

He was closing in, charging toward her like an angry bull.

Oh, God!

She pulled the key free, darted inside and flipped the latch on the dead bolt just as he raced up to the door. Now there was a locked barrier between them.

He yanked on the handle, making the glass vibrate.

What did he *want*?

Unable to get inside, he slapped the door. She backed away, watching him. He tilted his head to the side and looked the door over from top to bottom.

The movement was eerie, sending a chill over her skin.

Then he smashed his head against the door. Once. Twice. Under the force of the helmet, the glass splintered.

Melanie's heart clenched. She had to get to a phone. Call for help. Once the sheriff's department got the message, a deputy could be here in less than two minutes.

Unless that man reached her first.

The cracked webbing of the door spread. Panic zipped through her veins, hot as an electric current, driving her to move.

Melanie spun around and ran. Not to her office. If he knew who she was, and this wasn't some random attack, then he'd expect her to head there.

But where to go? None of the office doors locked.

Her pulse skittered. Her legs shook. Her mind raced even as time slowed to a crawl.

The glass shattered. He was coming. He was behind her and would erase the distance between them at a frightening rate.

She darted to the left, down a walkway. Her heel caught on the carpet. She tripped and fell hard, scraping her bare leg. As she climbed to her feet, a shoe came off. She surged forward, leaving the heel behind, and scanned the open cubicles where the legal assistants, witness advocates and interns worked. With only half walls dividing the section, hiding there, virtually out in the open, wasn't a possibility.

No time to hide. She had to call 911. Reaching over the half wall, she grabbed the receiver. Stabbed the number nine.

The next thing she knew, he was on her.

Strong hands flung her against the back wall and clamped around her throat. Melanie struggled and bucked to break free. Tried to throw another knee into that tender spot that would hurt him most.

But he turned at an angle, wedging one of his legs between her thighs. The stench of tobacco registered in her brain. She punched his forearms, hitting solid muscle, not making his grip budge in the least. Ice formed in her chest. She fought to get him off her. Every cell in her body strained with effort.

He had her, his hands locked in a viselike grip around her neck. She tried to scream. No air. Her lungs burned.

Fingers dug into her skin, pressing down on her windpipe, filling her with bone-deep fear. It felt as though her heart was being squeezed in a fist. He slammed the back of her head into the wall. The stunning blow shook her hands loose from his arms. He did it again.

Pain exploded in the back of her skull, blurring her vision. Tears stung her eyes. Much more of that and he'd knock her unconscious.

Melanie prayed he wasn't wearing steel-toed boots and thrust her remaining heel down onto his foot. He flinched.

His feet were vulnerable.

She stabbed the pointed heel down again with far more force. His hands loosened and he reared back a step. She kicked his shin, aiming the heel at bone, and threw a foot into his groin.

Turning, she fled. But she didn't make it far.

He pounced, tackling her to the floor. They wrestled, each struggling to gain the advantage. She threw an elbow into his throat.

Then she was scrambling up. And so was he.

The man threw her into the wall. His gloved hands seized her throat again. He maneuvered his lower half, pressing his knees between hers, protecting himself. His grip on her tightened, shutting off her airway.

A scream was strangled and died in her throat. She wanted

to ram the heel of her palm up into his nose to break it the way she'd been taught in self-defense class, but the helmet protected his face.

His face.

If she could see him, identify him, scratch him, claw his eyes, get his DNA under her nails in the event of a worst-case scenario in which she didn't make it out of this alive, that would be something.

A fierce sense of determination rushed through her veins. No matter what, she was going to take this guy down. Regardless of the personal cost.

Melanie resisted the instinct to pry his hands from her throat and reached for the visor. She shoved it, but the face shield didn't move. Like it had been glued shut.

One of his hands released the pressure against her windpipe. She sucked in a ragged breath.

A fist blasted into her jaw, knocking the air from her lungs. She reeled from the blow, but if he didn't like her messing with his face shield, then she had to get it up.

She scraped and clawed at the visor, prying her nails into the seam. Breaking several gel tips down to the nail bed, she forced a sliver of the dark tinted shield up. He slammed another fist into her.

Agony left her dazed and struggling to stay on her feet.

Letting her go, the man spun away, lowering his head, and adjusted the visor while she pressed herself against the wall, hauled in desperate breaths through the gut-wrenching pain and felt around for something, anything, to help her get out of this nightmare.

Her fingers grazed cold metal.

A fire extinguisher.

She unhooked it from the wall and swung the extinguisher like a baseball bat, smashing it into his head. He spun, thrown off balance. Not giving him a chance to recover, she rammed the butt of the extinguisher into his gut. She hit him again and again, this time over the back of the head, wanting to crack the helmet open.

He dropped to his knees and pitched forward, putting a hand to the floor to steady himself. She pulled the pin on the fire extinguisher, breaking the tamper seal, pointed the nozzle at him and squeezed the handle, spraying him with the extinguishing agent.

The man coughed and grunted.

Melanie spun on her heel and ran to the district attorney's office at the far end of the hall. She slammed the door shut behind her. Dropped the extinguisher. Grabbed a chair. Jammed the sturdy back under the lever door handle.

The next best thing to a lock.

But was it enough?

She hurried to the desk. Shoved it across the room with items on the top clattering to the floor. Pushed it against the door as a barricade.

Dread clogged her throat. She wiped moisture from her nose with the back of her trembling hand. Her face throbbed where he'd hit her, and her heart hammered against her ribs. She picked up the extinguisher and clutched it to her chest. Something inside of her needed to keep the makeshift weapon close.

She searched the floor and saw the landline phone.

On quivering legs, she stumbled to it, dropped to the floor in a shaking, terrified puddle and picked up the receiver.

Blood was on her hands, on the phone. Her blood.

Pressing her back to the desk, digging the heels of her feet into the carpet, pushing against it with all her weight to prevent him from getting inside the room, she dialed for help.

"This is nine-one-one, what's your emergency?"

Chapter Two

Detective Waylon Wright cut his gaze from the deputy assigned to do forensics working near Melanie's car and eyed the bouquet he'd sent her that had been trampled to pieces. He stalked toward the building, ducked under the crime-scene tape and headed down the short walkway.

At the shattered door, he stepped on broken glass, the shards crunching under his boots.

Entering the offices of the district attorney, he wiped away any trace of the feelings roiling through him from his face and walked down the hall. He was about to make a right toward Melanie's office, but he spotted the gaggle of deputies at the other end of the floor.

On his way down there, a spot in the hall caught his attention and he stopped. There were signs of a struggle and remnants of fire-extinguishing agent. He looked around before he made his way down to the DA's office. Deputies Cody and Lee blocked the threshold with their backs to the hall. Waylon put a hand on Lee's shoulder. The guy glanced at him and stepped aside, letting him through.

The office was in shambles. Melanie sat in a chair, an ice pack pressed to her cheek. An EMT was examining her. Mel's nose was bloody. The usual slick twist she wore was loose and messy, with wild black strands hanging around her face. She spoke in a firm, steady voice, giving a statement to chief deputy Holden Powell, who was crouched in front of her.

Waylon's mood darkened as he listened. Rage boiled inside him, his fingers curling into fists. But relief seeped through, too. She was alive.

"Once I managed to get away from him, I called nine-one-one." Mel's gaze flashed up to his. A flicker of unguarded emotion crossed her face, horror suddenly alive in the depths of her brown eyes. Tears glistened and one rolled down her cheek.

Looking away from him, she lowered her head and whisked the moisture from her eyes.

Holden glanced over at him and stood. "Waylon. What's the LPD doing here?"

"I was getting ready to head home, heard about the attack on the radio and the APB for the suspect." Not that the all-points bulletin had provided much to go on. Male. Dressed in all black. Wearing a dark tinted motorcycle helmet. Approximately six feet tall. Medium build. "Figured I'd swing by. Take a look around. Unofficially, of course. Make sure the town's favorite ADA is okay."

"Hope you're not planning to try and steal this case." Holden put his hands on his hips.

Melanie straightened. "I don't want him working on this one. He shouldn't even be here."

Gritting his teeth, Waylon gave a slow nod of acknowledgment. "As I was going to say, I had no intention of doing any such thing." Not that he could steal it even if he wanted to. This attack happened on the sheriff's turf. Literally. Made the case personal for them. It was personal for him as well, but Mel didn't want anyone to know that. Which he'd respect.

"Good," Holden said. "Then you're welcome to stay."

Thanks for your permission. He was staying whether Holden liked it or not.

"But we've got this well in hand," Holden added.

Waylon stepped deeper into the room. "No doubt in my mind you do. I'm here informally."

The chief deputy's gaze swung back to Melanie. "Did the assailant say anything to you? Threaten you? Indicate what he wanted?"

She shook her head. "No, he didn't."

"Not in the garage where he first attacked you," Holden said, "or here in the offices? Anything?"

"As a matter of fact, not a single word from him."

Holden made a note in his pad. "And when you managed to get his visor up, you didn't get a look at him at all? Could you see his skin color? Was he white, Black, Hispanic? What about his eye color?"

Taking a breath, Melanie shook her head again. "I don't know. Sorry. I tried to identify him, to get a sample of his DNA, but he had the visor glued shut. It took everything to get it up half an inch." Her gaze fell to the trembling hand in her lap.

Her fingernails were broken and bloody, her knuckles bruised. A bad scrape on her knee looked tender, and when the EMT cleaned the wound, Melanie flinched.

Waylon could only imagine how terrified she must've been, how hard she had fought to survive.

"After I got the visor to budge a little, it only enraged him. That's when he hit me." She gestured to her face, moved the ice pack from her left cheek and pressed it to the back of her head, giving him a good look at her.

A nasty bruise had already formed on her brown cheek. The ice had done little to prevent swelling. Blood oozed from a cut on her lower lip, and a black eye was blooming. He reckoned she was going to have one heck of a shiner in an hour or two.

Fury pierced Waylon deeply, taking root in a dark place inside him he seldom acknowledged. Melanie had taken brutal blows, but she didn't go down without a fight—fueled by fear and adrenaline, he supposed.

Weariness and pain glimmered in her eyes, right along with strength and determination. Tonight, he could've lost her forever. Regardless of whether they were together in some capacity, Melanie was a bright light, meant to shine and do so much good. The world would be a darker place without her.

He swore under his breath and swallowed around the lump of raw emotion lodged in his throat. The need to tear apart whoever had dared to hurt her surged through him, but he tamped it down.

"Any identifying marks?" Holden asked.

"He was completely covered. Helmet. Long sleeves. Gloves."

"Did you smell anything on him?" Waylon treaded closer. "Aftershave? Alcohol? Weed?"

Shooting him a fierce glance, Holden heaved a breath.

"Uh, yeah, I did." She nodded. "Cigarette smoke. Menthol."

"How can you be sure it was menthol?" the chief deputy asked.

Her father was a smoker. A bad habit she tried to get him to break.

"A guy I knew in Denver only smoked menthols. We spent a lot of time together. Sometimes the smell would get into my clothes."

They'd spent a lot of time together in close proximity if the smell permeated her clothing. News to him.

A lot about Melanie he longed to know, but only a brief window opened after they made love when she was willing to share. If she had to work the next day, once the sun rose, she threw on clothes, had coffee and either kicked him out of her house or she skedaddled from his place.

They'd been dancing that tango for almost three years. One night a week had turned into three, sometimes four. Strictly sex had shifted to takeout beforehand, cuddling afterward, along with pillow talk—a sure sign that things were more than physical—coffee together in the mornings and a few hurried kisses. Some holiday weekends they got to spend several days in a row together.

Fed up with the bare minimum, he'd finally pushed for a real relationship. He wanted to go out to dinner, hold her hand in public, take a vacation, wake up every day with her.

Discuss their future. The sex was off the charts. No woman did it for him the way she did. But he wanted more.

She didn't and had ended it. Lectured him about professional boundaries and spouted bad timing mumbo jumbo, in a rather cold and impersonal manner, like she was delivering a closing argument in a courtroom, without bothering to give him a chance at a rebuttal.

Deep down, he suspected she simply didn't want distractions from her job and was willing to burn any bridge to make district attorney.

Maybe she'd burned one too many bridges in Denver.

"Did the relationship end badly?" Waylon asked, eliciting another sigh from the chief deputy.

"It did." Melanie hung her head. "It's one of the reasons I moved here from Denver." The EMT bandaged her leg, and she winced. "But he wouldn't do this."

"Are you sure?" Holden asked and she nodded.

Waylon stepped within easy reach of her. "What's his name?"

Melanie stiffened, avoiding any eye contact.

"Give *me* his name," Holden said, throwing him a scathing glare. "*I'll* have a chat with him, feel him out. That way we can be sure and eliminate him as a possible suspect."

"That won't be necessary. You don't need his name." Her tone changed, the unyielding ADA coming through. "He isn't violent and has no cause to physically hurt me," she said to

Holden. "He was glad when I left Denver and we've had no contact since. This wasn't him."

Physically struck Waylon. This guy might want to hurt her emotionally. Or maybe she'd been the one hurt in the fallout of the relationship.

"Okay." Holden pressed his lips into a firm line. "Has anyone made any threats against you lately? Have you received any hate mail?"

Convicted felons sometimes said reckless things after sentencing, but he wasn't aware of anything recent, and he made it his business to keep track.

"Nothing. It's been quiet." Her delicate shoulders hunched. "Until tonight."

Another deputy pushed past the other two, entering the room holding a tablet. "The perp waited two hours for her." Deputy Platt turned the screen toward them and tapped it, playing back the surveillance footage from one of the security cameras.

Melanie got up from the chair and came over, standing between them. Her gaze fell to the tablet as her hand holding the ice pack lowered.

He looked at the side of her jaw. Swollen and quickly turning purple. His gut clenched as he imagined a meaty fist connecting with her face.

She stepped closer to him, on purpose or unconsciously, shifting his focus.

Waylon took in the scent of her. Jasmine and musk and something else warm that was particular to her. Whenever they were together at his place, he didn't wash his sheets immediately, just to hold on to the smell of her for as long as he could.

Their fingers brushed, the slight touch sending a spark shooting through him.

She moved her hand away, putting the cold compress back up to her face.

He guessed the contact had been purely accidental. But the proximity to Mel pulled at his emotions, a dangerous thing in a room full of people. He turned his attention back to the surveillance footage. Away from Melanie and the need he felt for her.

They watched the perp creep up the garage ramp, hugging the wall, to the third level. Helmet on. Gloves. Sneakers. He glanced at the cameras, like he already knew where they were located, and made a beeline for her car. Dropping down on the side out of view of the camera, he stayed there a moment and then crept over to one of the concrete pillars.

"Wonder why he decided to move so far away from her SUV and stopped there instead of hiding closer," Holden said, as if thinking aloud.

"Because of the position of the other two vehicles besides the ADA's still in the lot." Waylon pointed to them. "One of the drivers might have spotted him as they left."

The perp ducked down behind the pillar and took a seat on the ground. From that angle, with the low wall of the parking ramp that curved around as a shield, he was completely blocked from the view of the camera. The helmet lifted—he must've removed it, but they couldn't even see the top of his head to refine the description of who they were looking for.

Seconds later, a thin trail of smoke wafted up into the air from his position.

"He planned this out carefully," Waylon said. "Knew exactly where to hide and brought cigarettes to smoke while he waited. You need to have your deputies check the spot for cigarette butts and review all the footage for the last two or three weeks. Look for anyone scoping out the place, monitoring Mel—Merritt's—comings and goings."

"I know how to do my job," Holden said, the words emerging like a sigh. He looked at the deputies lingering in front of the door. "Go take care of it, will you?" He turned the tablet toward them, showing them where to look.

Cody hurried off down the hall.

Waylon would've apologized to Holden, but he wasn't sorry. He didn't care if he stepped on someone else's toes. This wasn't simply any case.

"I have no doubts about your competency or that of your department," Waylon said. "I just want to get this SOB. A dedicated detective should be helping you on this one." They were experts after all, and unlike the sheriff's department, they wouldn't have their focus spread thin by everything else going on in the entire county. This sort of thing would put a squeeze on their resources. The sheriff's department didn't even have the budget to keep crime-scene investigators on staff. A handful of their deputies had taken some training courses, making them capable of handling routine things such as thefts and burglaries. But their most experienced team member, who had worked homicides, had been killed recently. "Maybe Hannah Delaney, Kent Kramer or Brian Bradshaw." All were excellent, and more importantly, he trusted them.

"I'll give it consideration," Holden said. "Run the idea by the sheriff in the morning." He fast-forwarded the footage.

The perp finished smoking and put the helmet back on. The district attorney, Gordon Weisman, left a half hour later. At nine o'clock, one of the paralegals he recognized, Rosenfeld, walked out while talking on the phone. The young woman popped her trunk and rummaged around in the back for several minutes, engrossed in her conversation. No clue the guy was there, lurking only a few feet away. The woman hung up and climbed into her car.

Mel left the offices. She marched over to the trash can, hesitated a moment and threw away the flowers.

Waylon snuck a furtive look her way that she ignored without even a glance in his direction.

"Who were the flowers from?" Holden asked, pausing the playback.

"No one important," she said, her tone nonchalant. She tucked loose strands behind her ear, like a nervous habit.

He'd never seen the formidable Melanie Merritt nervous. Except for when he'd admitted his feelings for her.

"The guy is just an ex," she added, still fiddling with her hair. "Not even that. Simply someone I saw from time to time to scratch an itch, if you know what I mean, before I decided to end the dalliance."

No one important. Scratch an itch. Dalliance.

The words stung, wounding his heart more than his ego.

"The name of this spurned lover?" Holden held his pen, waiting for an answer.

"I never said *spurned.*"

"Maybe he didn't like you ending things," Holden said. "Maybe the message didn't sink in. Could be a situation where if he couldn't have you then no one could."

Waylon restrained a groan and swore to himself. He was about to make the list of suspects.

"He's a good guy," she said. "Not the perp you're after. Trust me."

The chief deputy folded his arms across his chest. "For a victim, you sure are reluctant to give us the names of these two men who could be responsible," he said, and her chin jerked up at that. "Nothing I can do about identifying Mr. Denver without your assistance. But Mr. Flowers is a different story. If there's a card from the shop out on the ground, it might have his prints."

Another curse prickled Waylon's tongue. It definitely had his prints.

"In the event it doesn't," Holden continued, "he probably used a credit card to pay for the flowers, or someone will remember him buying such an extravagant bouquet. We'll track him down with or without your cooperation, though I'd prefer the former."

Melanie pivoted, facing the chief deputy. "You're barking up the wrong tree. Any time you invest in looking into him is a waste. You should focus on anyone who seemed like they were surveilling the garage or monitoring my comings and goings, like Detective Wright suggested. Whoever attacked me obviously knew I leave late every night."

"Excuse me, ma'am," Cody said, coming back into the room, his hand outstretched. Her designer purse and leather laptop straps dangled from his fingers, and her shoe was in his other hand. "Here you go. You can have these back now and your wallet is in there."

"So, this wasn't a mugging." Waylon looked between Holden and Melanie. "I'm guessing that purse is worth a few hundred dollars." Not that he needed to guess. She'd spent more on some of her handbags than most folks in the area did on the monthly mortgage for their house. "And he didn't bother with your wallet. He targeted you and attacked you for some other reason."

Deputy Cody turned to Holden. "There were no cigarette butts in the spot where he hid. Only ash on the ground."

"If he was smart enough to pick it up and take it with him," Waylon said, "then surely he didn't send her flowers that could be traced back to him."

Holden frowned and it was obvious by the way his mouth twitched that the chief deputy was biting his tongue.

Melanie slipped on her second shoe. "Can I go now?" She stashed the ice pack in her purse. "If there are any other questions, I think it can wait until tomorrow. Don't you agree?"

Holden glanced past her at the EMT. "Is she medically cleared?"

"Are you sure you don't want to go get checked out at the hospital?" the tech asked.

She turned her attention to the EMT. "I'm good. Really. I need to get home."

"It's entirely possible you could have a concussion," the tech said.

"No blurred vision. No nausea. Or confusion. Or dizziness. If something changes, I'll go to the hospital. Right now, a trip to the emergency room is the last thing I want. I'm leaving."

The EMT shrugged and shut the lid to the first-aid kit. "I can't force you to take reasonable precautions, ma'am. You're cleared to leave if you want."

"I'll give you a ride home," Waylon said to her.

Melanie looked surprised. Then guarded. "Thanks, but I can drive myself."

"Afraid not, ma'am," Deputy Platt said.

Mel's brow furrowed. "Why is that?"

"When the perp dropped out of view on the side of your car, he flattened two tires," Waylon said. They had been slashed down to the rims. "He made sure you weren't going anywhere."

"We can give you a ride to your house," Holden said before Waylon had a chance to.

"No, no, that won't be necessary." She hitched her purse and laptop bag onto her shoulder. "You all have better things to do and it's late. I'll call for a rideshare. I'm fine."

Mel could be stubborn, but this wasn't the time for her obstinate independence.

"It is *late,* and you are *not* fine. You were just assaulted." Waylon marveled at her fierce determination to want to go home alone, in the dark, after what she had gone through. "I'm off duty." Which was relative. For him, he was always working. "I'll make sure you get home safely. Frees up the deputies so they can get back to work finding the guy who did this to you." He gave her an unflinching look to let her know this was nonnegotiable and stressed "Let's go." He extended his arm and waited for her to walk out first.

Her gaze narrowed, always a lawyer up for a fight, and he braced for her to debate the matter. Whether she liked it or not, she was going to be driven home. By him.

With an annoyed shake of her head, she left the office without protest.

In the hall, he came up beside her, but he didn't say anything until they had cleared the busted door. "Mel—"

She raised her palm, cutting him off. "Not here, Detective, and for the record, I'm capable of deciding how I get home."

Not wanting to argue, he walked her to his compact truck and unlocked the door. His GMC Sonoma was an older model that sat lower to the ground than newer trucks and lacked a running board. Putting his hands on her waist, he gave her a slight boost up inside since she was wearing a tailored slim-fitting skirt that restricted her movements.

Off to the side, he couldn't help noticing the card from the flower shop bagged as evidence.

Maybe it was best to have a frank conversation with Holden and tell him he'd been the former nobody in Melanie's bed. Sooner or later, Holden was going to find out anyway. But Waylon needed her permission first.

He hustled over to his side and took off. Once they cleared the garage, he glanced over at her. "Melanie."

"I know where this conversation is headed, and I don't want to have it."

If she thought he was going to bring up their former relationship, she was wrong. This wasn't the time or place for that kind of discussion. His only concern was her well-being and the case. "You've got no idea what I'm going to say."

"Your protective cowboy instincts are in overdrive right now because you have feelings for me."

"Apparently, they're one-sided."

"I didn't say that." She rubbed her temple. "I should've asked the medic for a painkiller for my head."

Waylon leaned over, popping the glove box, and handed her some Tylenol. His attention snagged on how her skirt rode up, exposing a bit of her sexy, toned thighs. Just enough silky-smooth, chestnut-colored skin to scatter his thoughts for a moment.

Clearing his head, he opened the center console and gave her a bottle of water. She dumped two gel capsules into her palm and washed them down with a little water.

"This conversation is going to get heavy. I don't want to say anything that'll hurt you," she said, but that was already too late. "Let's not do this right now. Okay?"

She phrased it like a question, as if it was up for discussion, but that wasn't the case. He was fluent in Mel-speak. She cracked her window several inches, letting in fresh air, and switched on the radio.

The sound of Garth Brooks crooning something about thunder rolling filled the truck cab and the empty space of silence between them.

His intent wasn't to cause more stress. They were going to discuss the way she'd blown up their relationship, but at a different time. Tonight, he only had one more thing that he had to mention. "In the morning, I need to tell Holden about us."

She opened her mouth to object.

"Stop." His voice was soft yet firm. "Listen to me. We both know it won't take him long to figure it out when he traces the flowers. But by then, he won't be the only one to know. The whole department will. I can get him to keep it quiet if I get out in front of it." He was on somewhat good terms with the Powell family these days. After he'd set aside old resentments with Holden's brother Monty and helped them all out on a mission across the state line, Waylon had earned the right to call in a favor. "I won't unless you agree, but it's the smart thing to do."

Melanie was brilliant. She had an uncanny ability to read

people, making her great at picking juries, spoke six different languages, attended a fancy prep school as a teen, went to Harvard and Yale, and was highly respected for her good judgment by most people he knew in law enforcement.

Once she eliminated emotion, she would see that this was the best way to handle it.

Flattening her mouth into a thin line, she simply nodded. "Are you sure he won't say anything?"

"Positive." Waylon frowned at the cut on her lip. When he got his hands on the guy who'd done that to her, he was going to make him regret it before he brought him to justice. There was no way he wasn't working on this case unofficially.

Officially, he needed to have a detective of his choice assigned to her case. The chief of the LPD, Wilhelmina Nelson, trusted his judgment, and if anyone could persuade Sheriff Daniel Clark, it was her, considering they were married.

In what felt like no time, they turned down Melanie's street. She only lived fifteen minutes away in a house on a cul-de-sac, in a quiet, middle-class neighborhood that had good-size yards, with decent space between the homes.

Waylon parked in the driveway. He was out of his truck and by her passenger's side door when she stepped onto the asphalt with her bags.

"I'll check inside before you go in," he said.

"If you insist."

"I do." He was grateful she didn't argue with him. They headed for her covered front steps. "I can stay the night if you want," he offered, and she tensed. "On the sofa or in the guest room, Mel." Goodness, he didn't want her to think he was trying to make a move on her at a time like this. She'd just gone through something traumatic and needed to rest without worry. "It's not good for you to be alone tonight. I'd prefer to be inside instead of sleeping in my truck, parked in your driveway." But he wasn't leaving her alone.

"You should go home." She tucked more strands behind her ear. "I don't need a babysitter, especially not…" Her voice trailed off as she stopped near the steps.

He tore his gaze from her face and looked to see what she was staring at.

On her front stoop under the portico, there was a circle of sand. Two feet in diameter. In the center was an impression, resembling an angel. Like someone had made it in the sand using a large doll.

"I-i-it can't be," she whispered, her face growing ashen. "It can't be."

"Mel, what are you talking about? Can't be what?"

Shaking her head slowly, she suddenly looked terrified. "It's not possible. I made sure he was convicted and put him behind bars."

"Who?" Waylon looked back at the front stoop. "What is this?"

"He swore he'd make me pay. Me and everyone else responsible for his conviction." She started trembling. "But he's serving a life sentence in a Colorado prison. It can't be him. He couldn't be the one who attacked me."

Waylon took hold of her shoulders, turning her toward him. "Who are you talking about?" he asked gently.

She swallowed so hard it was audible. "That's his calling card." She pointed back at the stoop while staring at him, her eyes filling with tears. "Drake Colter. The Sand Angel Killer."

Available soon wherever
Harlequin Books are sold.